Book 7: Target

Also by Chris Bradford

The Bodyguard series
Book 1: Recruit
Book 2: Hostage
Book 3: Hijack
Book 4: Ransom
Book 5: Ambush
Book 6: Survival
Book 7: Target
Book 8: Traitor

BODYGUARD

Book 7: Target

Chris Bradford

Philomel Books

PHILOMEL BOOKS
an imprint of Penguin Random House LLC
375 Hudson Street, New York, NY 10014

Copyright © 2016, 2018 by Chris Bradford.
First American edition published by Philomel Books in 2018. Adapted from
Target, originally published in the United Kingdom by Puffin Books in 2016.
Penguin supports copyright. Copyright fuels creativity, encourages diverse
voices, promotes free speech, and creates a vibrant culture. Thank you for
buying an authorized edition of this book and for complying with copyright
laws by not reproducing, scanning, or distributing any part of it in any form
without permission. You are supporting writers and allowing Penguin to
continue to publish books for every reader.
Philomel Books is a registered trademark of Penguin Random House LLC.

Library of Congress Cataloging-in-Publication Data is available upon request.
Printed in the United States of America.
ISBN 9781524739355
10 9 8 7 6 5 4 3 2 1

American edition edited by Brian Geffen.
American edition design by Jennifer Chung.
Text set in 11-point Palatino Nova.
This is a work of fiction. Names, characters, places, and incidents either are the
product of the author's imagination or are used fictitiously, and any
resemblance to actual persons, living or dead, businesses, companies, events,
or locales is entirely coincidental.

To my goddaughter, Lucinda—

Always there for you

"The best bodyguard is the one nobody notices."

With the rise of teen stars, the intense media focus on celebrity families and a new wave of millionaires and billionaires, adults are no longer the only target for hostage-taking, blackmail and assassination—kids are too.

That's why they need specialized protection . . .

GUARDIAN

Guardian is a secret close-protection organization that differs from all other security outfits by training and supplying only young bodyguards.

Known as guardians, these highly skilled kids are more effective than the typical adult bodyguard, who can easily draw unwanted attention. Operating invisibly as a child's constant companion, a guardian provides the greatest possible protection for any high-profile or vulnerable young target.

In a life-threatening situation, a **guardian** is the final ring of defense.

PREVIOUSLY ON BODYGUARD . . .

Guardian recruit Connor Reeves has encountered terrorist attacks, pirate hijackings and military coups during his assignments as a young bodyguard, but he wouldn't have survived without help . . .

"Hi, Connor, it's Charley," said a voice on the line. "Intelligence reports a suspected car bomb has gone off at H Street and Ninth."

"That's near Secret Service headquarters!"

"We know. The explosion was detonated right outside the entrance. Hang on—" There was a ping of an incoming message and a muffled gasp. "There's been a *second* explosion, near the Capitol Building this time."

"I just heard it," said Connor, the tourists milling around him still oblivious.

"Get off the streets now!"

———

Charley Hunter is operations leader for Alpha team and the one Guardian recruit Connor can always rely on . . .

"Don't stop," urged Charley.

Connor kept his foot firmly on the accelerator, but the scraping between the cars was like fingernails being clawed down a chalkboard. Then, with a final *screech*, they were beyond the roadblock.

Charley looked back out of the rear window. "Don't worry, it was just your front bumper falling off!" she said, keeping her voice light and breezy.

———

Charley is always the last person to wish him farewell before a mission . . .

With a final thumbs-up to his teammates, Connor started to close the door, but Charley reached in and touched his arm.

"Try not to catch any bullets this time," she said.

Connor gave her a quizzical look. "Surely that's the point of a bodyguard."

Charley locked eyes with him. "*Only* if all else fails."

———

And when all else does fail, Charley is the first person Connor calls . . .

"Charley, you have to listen to me," interrupted Connor,

his voice sounding strained. "I've just been captured. I've been given twenty-four hours to live. Emily is . . ."

The line crackled and Connor's voice was lost.

Charley pressed the phone to her ear. "Connor! Are you still there?"

———

For during the course of their training, Charley and Connor have grown close . . .

Charley began to bite her nails. She felt partly responsible for Connor's fate. She was the operations leader, after all. An ominous thought passed through her mind. *Perhaps bad karma's following me since my last assignment as an active guardian.* Nothing, it seemed, had gone right for her since that fateful day. Connor had been a turning point in her life, or so she had hoped. But now it appeared he would be yet another dead end. Literally.

———

Yet Connor knows little about Charley's past, despite his questioning . . .

"Tell me, why's your shield gold?"

Charley glanced down at the badge on her chest. "These are awarded for outstanding bravery in the line of duty."

Intrigued, Connor asked, "What did you do?"

Charley stopped by the window and looked out at the mountains in the distance.

"As guardians, we hope for the best but plan for the worst," she said softly. "Sometimes, the worst happens."

———

So now the time has come for Charley to finally open up to him . . .

"I want to know," said Connor, sitting down next to her. "I want to know everything about you."

Taking a deep breath, Charley steeled herself to revisit her past. "Well . . . This is the first time that I've ever told anyone the full story . . ."

Read on to discover Charley's thrilling path to becoming a Guardian . . .

PROLOGUE

The hot California sun glinted off the SUV's hubcaps as it cruised along the quiet suburban street. The man behind the wheel spotted a schoolgirl skipping on the sidewalk, his attention caught by her ponytail of golden-blond hair flicking from side to side. Judging from the carefree bounce in her step, she was no more than ten years old.

With a quick glance in his rearview mirror, the driver slowed down. He was almost alongside the girl when a voice cried out, "Charlotte!"

She stopped and turned. Another girl, petite with almond-shaped eyes, emerged from the porch of a large house. Her pink backpack rode high on her shoulders as she ran across the sunbaked lawn.

"*Ni hao*, Kerry!" Charlotte called back.

Her friend smiled warmly, revealing a set of braces. "Hey, your Chinese is getting good."

"I've been practicing," said Charlotte as the SUV continued past, unnoticed.

"You want to learn some more?" Kerry asked.

"Yeah," Charlotte replied eagerly. "We could use it as a secret code at school."

Kerry moved closer and whispered, "A best-friend language." She held up her little finger. "Friends forever?"

Charlotte entwined her own little finger around Kerry's. "Friends forever."

Then, hand in hand, they set off down the road. At the junction, the silver SUV with tinted windows pulled up in front of them, and the passenger door swung open.

"Excuse me, girls," said the driver with a forlorn look. "Can you help me? I'm a bit lost."

They both stared at the man, taking in his bald head, reddened cheeks and beginnings of a double chin. Intrigued by his accent, Charlotte asked, "Are you from England?"

The man nodded. "I'm on vacation. I'm supposed to meet my daughter at Disneyland, but I got off the highway at the wrong exit."

"You really are lost," said Kerry. "Disneyland's in Anaheim. You're in North Tustin."

The man sighed and shook his head at the map on the passenger seat. "American roads! They're almost as wide as they are long. Can you show me exactly where I am?"

"Sure," said Kerry, leaning in to look at the map.

The man's eyes lingered briefly on Charlotte. Then he turned his full attention to Kerry.

Charlotte noticed an illuminated screen on the dashboard. "Why not use your GPS?" she suggested.

The man responded with a tight smile. "Can't work it for the life of me. Rental car."

Charlotte's eyes narrowed. His explanation was unconvincing; even her dad could work a GPS. "Kerry, I think we should be go—"

Before Kerry could move, the man rammed a stun gun against her neck. Kerry shrieked, her body juddering with a million volts. Her eyes rolled back and she fell limp. The man seized Kerry's backpack straps and, with a vicious tug, wrenched her body into the interior of the car.

Shocked by the speed of the attack, Charlotte stood rooted to the spot. She didn't try to grab Kerry, or even call for help. She just watched as the door slammed shut on her best friend. Then the SUV shot off, sped around a corner and disappeared.

1

Four years later . . .

Charley gazed at the thin line of horizon separating sea and sky. In the sun's warm summer glow, she waited for the tell-tale ripple that would swell into the perfect wave to ride. Yet, as the ocean lapped gently against her surfboard, a shudder of uneasiness swept through her.

On instinct, she glanced around, but saw only other surfers bobbing on the water, each biding their time for the next decent wave. Charley shook the dark feeling away and focused on the horizon. She was determined not to let old memories surface and cloud the rest of her day.

She surfed to forget.

Out on the water, the rest of the world disappeared. It was just her, the board and the waves.

In the distance a ripple grew into a promising swell. Charley splashed salt water in her face and ran her hands through her damp sun-bleached hair to clear her mind. Then she heard a name she thought she'd left behind for good.

"Hey, Charlotte!" called a voice. "Charlotte Hunter?"

Charley turned to see a young, tanned surfer paddle up beside her. No one had called her Charlotte since she'd moved from North Tustin to San Clemente on the coast.

"It *is* you," he declared, sitting up on his board. A mop of tousled sandy hair half covered his eyes, but stopped short of concealing the easy smile that greeted her gaze. A couple of years older than Charley, he wore a tight black vest that emphasized his impressive muscles.

Good-looking as he was, Charley didn't recognize him. "Sorry, you've got me confused with someone else," she said.

The young surfer studied her a moment longer. "No, it *is* you," he insisted. "I saw you a couple of summers back at the Quiksilver surf championships. You were awesome! Totally deserved to win. Takes some serious skills to pull off those turns. And that final kickflip was sick!"

Blindsided by his praise, Charley mumbled thanks, then returned her attention to the approaching swell.

"So, where have you been hiding?" he asked, not taking the hint. "After you won, you kinda dropped off the radar."

Charley's gaze didn't waver from the horizon and she kept the grief from her voice. "My parents died in a plane crash."

The surfer opened then closed his mouth, the lapping of the sea and the breaking of waves on the shoreline filling the awkward silence.

It took all of Charley's willpower to suppress the despair

that threatened to engulf her. If losing her best friend wasn't enough, her parents had been killed during a terrorist hijacking of a passenger jet only two years after Kerry's kidnapping. The double tragedy had almost broken her.

Charley desperately willed her wave closer. She needed to be in its pocket, surfing at the edge of her ability, where thoughts of her parents—and of Kerry—were drowned out by the sheer power of the ocean.

"No offense, but I like to surf alone," she said, circling her board around in readiness to catch the oncoming wave.

"Sure . . . I understand," said the young surfer breezily. "But if you want to hang out sometime, we're having a beach party tomorrow night. My name's Bud—" An urgent honking of car horns from the coastal road interrupted his flow. "What's got them so freaked?"

Then they both spotted a huge gray dorsal fin cutting through the waves.

A lifeguard's cry of "SHARK!" sent a spike of fear through every surfer in the water.

"Let's bail!" said Bud, paddling furiously for the shoreline with every other sane surfer.

But Charley remained where she was. Shark or no shark, she intended to wait for *her* wave. It was a beauty—powerful, glassy and promising a perfect A-frame break. She figured riding the wave would be safer and quicker than madly paddling for the shore. But if she was going to be shark bait, then so be it. In her experience of life so far, she'd learned that fate had already dealt the cards. She couldn't change the outcome. That fact didn't make her any less scared of the shark. Just realistic.

She watched the ominous fin slice through the water, then disappear beneath the surface. The presence of the predator at least explained her earlier unease.

With the swell rolling in behind her, Charley began to paddle. She felt the rise of the ocean and the intense energy of the wave building. A familiar thrill pulsed through her veins as her board rapidly picked up speed . . . Then, just as she was popping to her feet, the shark broke the surface. It was a great white, over ten feet long.

Charley almost wiped out. Only now did she regret letting her stubborn need to surf override her survival instinct. But the shark wasn't interested in her. Its target was a young boy on a longboard much closer to shore. Charley watched in mute horror as the great white bore down on its prey, opening its formidable jaws and sinking its teeth into both boy and board before dragging them under.

Recovering her balance, Charley took the drop down the wave. It was a clean break, offering a safe run all the way to the beach . . . but she made a snap decision to change her line when the boy popped up again. Screaming for help, he was still caught in the jaws of the great white, only his longboard preventing him from being torn apart.

She carved her way toward him. She figured she had a slim chance of saving the boy if she could time her descent to collide directly into the shark's head.

Charley had just a second to realize how crazy her stunt was before the tip of her board struck the shark with such force that she flipped over the top. Somersaulting through the air, she plunged headfirst into the sea. The wave broke hard, barreling everything along in its path. Charley was spun over and over. Water roared in her ears. For one horrifying moment she believed she might never surface again. Then the mighty wave passed and her head bobbed up in the foaming water.

Gasping for breath, she searched around for the boy. By some miracle her insane plan had worked. The great white had released its death grip, and the boy was floundering a few yards away, blood pouring from his wounds. Retrieving her board on its leash, Charley paddled hard toward him. She could see the great white circling for another attack.

"Take my hand!" she cried.

The boy weakly reached out, and Charley pulled him to her just as the enraged shark exploded out of the water. The great white missed the boy by an inch, its jaws clamping down onto his longboard instead. Still attached by the leash, the boy was almost torn from her grip. Charley snatched the small dive knife strapped to her ankle and cut the plastic line.

With blood swirling in the sea, the great white whipped into a frenzy. Within seconds the creature had shredded the longboard to pieces, and then its cold black eyes turned to Charley. Suppressing a stab of panic, she grabbed the flailing boy and hauled him onto her own board.

"Hold tight," she told him as the next wave rolled in.

Kicking hard, Charley body-surfed toward the beach. The wave bore them all the way, mercifully dumping them both in the shallows. Four surfers ran in and dragged them the last few feet to the safety of the shore. Once on the beach, the lifeguard began emergency medical treatment on the boy.

"Call an ambulance!" he ordered one of the surfers.

"Will he live?" asked Charley, getting shakily to her feet. She was breathless and her heart pounded. Bystanders were asking if she was all right, but she waved them away.

"I think so," the lifeguard replied as he stemmed the boy's blood loss. "Thanks to you."

Charley nodded, then retrieved her board and quietly disappeared into the gathering crowd.

2

Having washed the blood off herself and her board, Charley sat down on a secluded sand dune to inspect the damage. Not to her own body, which had escaped with only a few scrapes and bruises, but to her precious surfboard. Remarkably, the board had survived the encounter with the great white. Only the nose had suffered a bad ding. *That'll cost a lot to get repaired*, she thought. But money was not the problem, as long as her foster parents allowed her access to the trust-fund account.

For the time being, Charley sealed the damage with some epoxy resin from her board bag. As she squeezed the tube's contents over the ding, she noticed her hands were trembling and realized her fixation on the board must be the result of deep shock. She had no idea what had possessed her to tackle a great white head-on. It had been insane!

Yet, despite the terrifying encounter, she also felt strangely elated. For the first time in her life, she'd confronted death . . . and won.

How Charley wished she'd possessed some of that courage during Kerry's abduction. There wasn't a day that she didn't think of her friend. Despite the statewide search by police and all the publicity, Kerry had never been found. Nor had her abductor.

For the past four years, Charley had replayed the nightmare scene over and over in her head. How the situation could have been different if only she'd acted on her instinct sooner. If only she'd offered to look at the map. If only she'd reached out and grabbed her friend. If only she'd screamed for help. If only she'd taken down the vehicle's license plate number. *If only* . . .

Tears welling in her sky-blue eyes, Charley forced herself to take several deep breaths. She swallowed the sharp pain of her grief that never seemed to dull with time. Gradually the trembling subsided and she regained control.

While she waited for the resin to dry, Charley sat in the dunes, knees hugged to her chest, and stared out at the limitless expanse of the Pacific Ocean. Gulls flew overhead in a cloudless blue sky. Bright sunshine glinted off emerald-green waters. And glassy waves, now abandoned and free of surfers, peeled along the coast in perfect white lines. The sight was breathtaking.

There was no indication that a deadly predator swam just beneath the surface.

Just like it is in life, thought Charley bitterly.

"Thinking of going back out?" inquired a deep gravelly voice.

Charley snapped her head around to see a man cresting the dune. She raised a hand to shield her eyes from the sun. The stranger was tall and broad with close-cut silver-gray hair. Despite wearing a faded O'Neill T-shirt and board shorts, he was no surfer. A camera dangled around his neck where a long white scar cut a jagged line across his throat. But it was the man's English accent that put her most on guard.

"Maybe," she replied tersely.

The man raised a questioning eyebrow. "You have a death wish?"

Charley shrugged. "At least I'd get the waves to myself."

The stranger grunted a laugh, then glanced at the beach where the injured boy was being transferred into an ambulance, its lights flashing. A TV news camera crew was now filming the scene.

"That was a remarkable act of courage," he said. "Everyone else fled, but you surfed right into the danger zone. Did you know the boy?"

Charley shook her head.

"So why risk your life saving a stranger?" he pressed.

Charley was uncomfortable with this personal line of questioning. "I don't know," she replied honestly, then narrowed her eyes. "I suppose I don't like the strong taking advantage of the weak."

The man seemed to smile at this. "And why walk away? You could be basking in the limelight, rather than sheltering alone in this dune."

"I don't like attention," Charley replied.

"That's good," said the stranger, taking a step closer. "Nor do I."

Charley tensed, growing ever more fearful of the man's intentions.

"What's your name?" he asked.

"What's it to you?" Charley shot back.

Pointing to his camera, the man replied, "I'm not a reporter, if that's what you're thinking."

"That's *not* what I'm thinking."

The man studied her intently, his flint-gray eyes finally coming to rest on her damaged board. "I can see you want to be left alone."

With that, he tipped his finger to his brow by way of good-bye, then strolled off. As he disappeared over the dune, Charley relaxed her grip on the dive knife she'd kept concealed beneath the board. Only when she was convinced he had gone did she slide its blade back into its sheath.

3

"*Don't* lie to us!" snapped Jenny, Charley's foster mother. "We know you weren't at school. We just spoke to your homeroom teacher."

Charley stared sullenly at the bare wooden floor of her foster parents' house. She'd known it was only a matter of time—her truancy was bound to come out. The shark attack had been all over the local news when she'd come home the previous evening, and speculation was rife about the mystery surfer girl. During a TV news report, Bud had been interviewed, and Charley's heart had jumped into her mouth. The last thing she'd wanted was her foster parents to know that she'd skipped school to surf. And although Bud had kept her identity to himself—for which Charley was grateful—her foster parents had still guessed, resulting in yet another argument in their "happy" home.

"You could have been killed!" said Bob, her foster father, glaring at her from beneath his bushy eyebrows.

"But I wasn't," Charley mumbled, wondering how two puritanical churchgoers could only focus on her lies and not the fact that she'd saved someone's life.

Jenny folded her arms. "You're not going surfing ever again."

Charley looked up in horror. "You can't take that from me," she begged.

"Yes, we can. You know how we feel about *surfing*." She said the word like it was a vulgar term. "It leads to immoral and sinful behavior—as your persistent truancy and dishonesty proves."

"Your board's going in the garbage," Bob agreed with finality.

Charley's mouth fell open. Surfing was the lifeline that kept her going. Overcome with fury, she screamed, "I wish *you* were dead and *not* my parents!"

Storming out of the hallway, she slammed the front door on them, then stood, fists clenched and body shuddering, on the porch. From the other side of the door, she heard Jenny cry, "The Lord Almighty give me strength! Why do we even bother? She's a lost cause."

"We must remind ourselves Charley's been through a lot," said Bob. "We need to make allowances."

"We're *always* making allowances while *she* puts us through misery! I've lost count of the number of times she's lied, skipped school and been in trouble with the police. What I'd give to see the back of her."

Bob sighed. "If that's how you feel, my love, then perhaps it's time we spoke with the social worker about rehoming her. Let's talk more when you get back from work . . ."

Charley blinked away the sting of tears. She knew she'd never made it easy for them. The fact was they simply couldn't understand her. They weren't her parents, never would be. But to be treated like some dog to be "rehomed" cut deep, and her heart hardened against her foster parents.

Charley strode down the driveway, kicking over one of Jenny's prized potted plants. As she reached the road, she noticed a white SUV with tinted windows parked a little way from her foster parents' house. Charley couldn't be certain, but she thought she'd seen the same vehicle the night before. White SUVs were commonplace in her neighborhood, but this particular one had cruised up and down as if the driver had been looking for someone. At the time, Charley had thought it might be a freelance reporter scouting for the mystery surf girl. But its continued presence this morning raised alarm bells.

As she crossed the street in the direction of her school, Charley casually glanced over her shoulder and made a mental note of the SUV's license plate—6GDG468. She wasn't taking any chances. After Kerry's abduction, her parents had become understandably overprotective. For the first few months, they hadn't let her out of their sight, but eventually they realized she needed more freedom to have a normal life. So the compromise had been for Charley to take self-defense classes and a street-awareness course. One of the key lessons had been to stay alert for unusual behavior or repeated sightings of people and vehicles.

As she reached the next junction, Charley looked up and down the road for traffic. But she was only interested in spotting one vehicle: the white SUV.

There was no sign of it and Charley relaxed. Evidently her gut reaction had been wrong. Heading across the road and down the hill, she wondered how to persuade her foster parents to let her out that evening for Bud's beach party. She wanted to thank him for keeping her name out of the news. But there was no way they'd give permission. Not at her age and especially after their last argument. She could say she'd been invited to a friend's sleepover, but she was probably grounded for life—if she wasn't already rehomed, that was! She'd just have to sneak out when they went to bed.

Charley waited at a set of traffic lights for the pedestrian signal to turn green. Several vehicles pulled up. The fifth in line was a white SUV. Charley clocked the license plate— 6GDG468—and felt her pulse quicken. Could it be a coincidence? The road did lead to the highway, after all. But, to rule out any possibility of being followed, Charley took a left instead of going straight on and cut across a small park to a residential road that ran parallel to the highway.

The route was clear, but then she spotted the SUV turning into *her* road. Charley quickened her pace, her heart thumping. The advice from her street-awareness course on being followed was to head for a populated area and find a safe location—a friend's house, a police station, a restaurant or a library. Charley hurried into downtown San Clemente, a wide tree-lined boulevard with mom-and-pop stores on either side. They were just opening, so only a handful of early-morning shoppers could be seen.

Charley stopped outside a hair salon. She needed a good look at the driver to confirm her suspicions without him knowing, so she pretended to study the beauty products on offer. In the reflection of the salon's window, she watched as the white SUV rolled down the street and parked in one of the spots on the opposite side of the road. No one got out.

Charley felt eyes upon her, and a shiver ran down her spine. The driver's face was obscured by a tinted windshield, but she could make out a bald head. Her throat tightened as an old fear gripped her heart: the man who'd taken Kerry had finally come back for *her*!

Seized by a panic attack, Charley half walked, half ran down the street. Her foster mother worked in the community center near the pier. If she could just reach there, she'd feel safer. Charley risked a glance back. The driver was getting out. He was stocky with a short goatee and pale skin, the lack of suntan confirming he was no local. Dark sunglasses concealed his features, and Charley's memory of the kidnapper's face was hazy after so many years. But one thing was certain—this man was following her.

With her attention distracted, Charley ran headlong into the arms of another man.

"Whoa, slow down!" he said, grabbing hold of her wrist as she stumbled back from the impact.

Charley stared into the flinty eyes of the stranger she'd met on the dunes.

"We just want to talk, Charley," he said, jutting his jaw at the bald man approaching from behind. Now Charley was even more spooked. *He knows my name!*

"Get off me!" she cried, spinning her wrist to break his grip and kicking him hard in the shins, just as she'd been taught in self-defense class.

The man grunted in pain and let go. Charley sprinted past him and across the street, only to collide into someone leaving a coffee shop. A fresh cappuccino and sugared doughnut went flying.

"*What the heck!*" cried Deputy Sheriff Jay Valdez as he shook hot coffee from his hands and inspected his stained uniform.

"Thank God," said Charley, grabbing hold of the officer. "I'm being followed!"

The deputy looked beyond her and across the street, a dubious frown on his face. "By who exactly?"

Charley spun around. There was no sign of the SUV. The stranger and his accomplice had seemingly vanished into thin air.

4

"We've talked about this before, Charley," said Deputy Valdez as he sat opposite her in one of the coffee shop's red leather booths. "You can't keep skipping school."

"But I was being followed," Charley insisted, a frothy hot chocolate cupped between her hands.

"So *that's* your excuse this time?" The deputy sighed and put down the napkin he'd been using to mop up his uniform. With a kindly smile, he continued, "I know you've had a troubled past and it can't be easy for you, but you need to shape up, Charley. You've got your whole life ahead of you. Don't throw it all away just because you've had a rough start."

"A rough start!" Charley gripped her cup so tightly she thought it might crack. "My best friend abducted and my parents killed in a plane hijacking. How much rougher can it get? I'm sorry if I'm not exactly looking forward to the rest of my life!"

Valdez propped his elbows on the table and leaned

forward. "Listen to me, Charley. We cannot change the cards we are dealt, just how we play the hand."

Charley stared into the dark depths of her hot chocolate. "What's that supposed to mean?"

"That it's not life's challenges or setbacks that define who we are. It's how we *react* to them that defines us," he explained. "You have a choice. You can give up and let life defeat you—or you can rise up and become stronger."

"That's easy enough for you to say," she mumbled.

"Yes, it is. Because I know all about rough starts." Valdez tugged back the sleeve of his uniform to reveal a small faded tattoo of a five-pointed crown on his inner wrist. "When I was your age, I was in a street gang."

Charley glanced up in surprise.

"Drugs, drink, violence, guns. That was my world as a boy. My brother got killed in a fight during a turf war. Then my life spiraled out of control . . . until a police officer arrested me. But he didn't take me to the station; instead he took me back home and told me exactly what I've just said to you." He fixed her with his brown-flecked eyes. "His advice changed my life. I can only hope it changes yours too."

Uncertain how to respond, Charley continued staring at the froth in her cup. The deputy's words had struck a nerve deep inside her. But she had no idea where to begin, or even if she had the strength to fight back against life's challenges.

"You have real potential, Charley, if only you'd apply it,"

Valdez encouraged. "I know Bob and Jenny are at their wits' end with you. Don't you want to make them proud of you?"

"What do they care? They're not my parents."

"No, but they're good people, trying to do right by you. And you're not making their lives any easier with your truancy and storytelling."

"I *wasn't* making it up!"

"Okay, I believe you," replied the deputy, holding up his hands. He tapped a finger to the notepad in his pocket. "I'll look into the license plate you've given me. Just promise to think about what I've said."

"Sure," agreed Charley, relieved that he was at last taking some action.

Deputy Valdez reclined in his seat and gazed out of the window. "You wouldn't happen to know who rescued that boy from the shark attack yesterday, would you?"

"No . . . I don't know what you're talking about," said Charley, taken off guard by the sudden change in topic.

Valdez looked sideways at her, a knowing smile on his lips. "See what I mean? Potential. Don't waste it."

The door to the coffee shop opened. A customer walked in and seated himself in a booth by the front window. Charley almost spilled her drink. She leaned across the table and hissed under her breath to Valdez. *"That's one of the men I was telling you about."*

The deputy glanced over at the silver-haired man by the

window. Sitting ramrod straight, the stranger gave the appearance of someone not to be messed with. He looked in his midforties, but had the body of a much younger man. And, while he wore a fancy suit, his craggy face and the visible scar around his neckline told of a more violent past.

"Okay, let me speak to him," said Valdez, rising from his seat. "You stay here."

The deputy strode across to the stranger and stood over him, his hand resting lightly upon the gun on his hip. Charley was too far away to hear their conversation, but she saw the stranger hand over his ID. Valdez inspected it, then raised an inquiring eyebrow. The stranger passed Valdez a file. The deputy flicked through it. They talked for several minutes, Charley growing more concerned with each passing second. Then Valdez handed back the documents and, to Charley's astonishment, saluted the man.

Valdez returned to Charley's booth, the expression on his face unreadable. "I think you should hear what he has to say."

5

Charley nervously settled herself in the seat opposite the stranger. Deputy Sheriff Valdez remained at the coffee bar, a discreet distance away but within earshot. His continued presence reassured Charley, but her heart still raced. What did this scarred man want?

"What I'm about to discuss with you is highly classified," said the stranger, his hands folded over a mysterious brown folder on the table. "In the interests of national security, you're not to discuss this with *anyone*. Understood?"

Charley swallowed uneasily and a shiver ran down her spine. Whatever this man wanted with her, it was serious. She gave a hesitant nod.

"My name is Colonel Black. I head up a close-protection organization known as Guardian—a covert independent agency with ties to the British government's security and intelligence service—"

"Am I in danger?" Charley interrupted, her chest tightening.

"Far from it," he replied with a steely smile. "In fact, you're the sort of person we're looking for to protect others from danger."

Charley frowned, her anxiety now replaced by confusion. *Me?* What are you talking about?"

"I'm here to recruit you as a bodyguard."

Charley burst into laughter. She half expected a cameraman to pop out, with a zany host announcing she was on a prank TV show. "You can't be serious!"

"Deadly serious," he replied, his gaze unwavering.

From the severe expression on his face, Charley got the sense this colonel wasn't the sort of man who made jokes often, if at all. She glanced over at Valdez for confirmation. The deputy sheriff nodded; evidently he'd been convinced by the man's credentials. But if this information was classified, Charley wondered what exactly Colonel Black had told the deputy.

"You do realize I'm just a kid," she told the colonel.

"The best bodyguard is the one nobody notices," he replied. "That's why young people like yourself make exceptional bodyguards."

"But I thought all bodyguards were ripped, muscular guys. I'm a girl, in case you hadn't noticed."

"That gives you a distinct advantage," said the colonel. "A female bodyguard can blend into any crowd and is often mistaken for a friend or work associate of the Principal—the person she's been assigned to protect. But she can drop you with an elbow or a roundhouse punch faster than you could shake somebody's hand. As I said, the best bodyguard is one nobody notices—which makes girls among the very best."

Charley's head was spinning. This was beyond anything she'd expected. If not a potential stalker, she'd assumed the stranger might be an official from social services. But the head of a secret bodyguard agency!

"Why *me*?" she eventually asked.

"You've proved you have the skills and talent."

Charley blinked. "I have?"

"Rescuing that boy from the shark was evidence of your courage," he explained. "Willingness to risk your own life for another is a crucial factor in being a bodyguard."

"But that was stupid of me . . . I wasn't even thinking."

"No, you were acting on your natural instinct."

"But I'm *not* bodyguard material," insisted Charley.

"Really?" challenged the colonel, his flint-gray eyes narrowing. "What's the license plate number of the white SUV?"

"Um . . . 6GDG468," Charley answered, thrown by the sudden switch in topic.

"When did you first notice the vehicle?"

"On my foster parents' street."

"And when did you realize it was following you?"

"At the traffic lights."

"What did the driver look like?"

"Bald, slightly overweight, with a goatee. Why all these questions?"

"That follow was set up to test your observation skills. And it's clear you've passed with flying colors—"

"You're saying that was a *test*?" Charley cut in, her earlier panic now turning to anger.

"Yes. The man who tailed you is named Bugsy," the colonel revealed, pointing through the window to her "stalker" leaning against the hood of the re-parked SUV. He gave Charley a little wave. "Bugsy is the surveillance tutor for our recruits."

"I don't care if he's the president of the United States of America, I won't forgive him for scaring the hell out of me!" Charley snapped.

"You also employed some excellent anti-surveillance techniques, especially the use of reflections in the shop window. That's another core set of skills a bodyguard needs," the colonel explained. "And it's evident you know martial arts from the damage you inflicted on my shin!"

Charley offered a wry smile. The shin kick was her one small victory in the whole setup. "Sorry about that," she said with a blatant lack of sympathy.

"No need to apologize," he replied drily. "Your reaction was reassuringly quick and effective. Are you still training?"

Charley shook her head. "No, I quit the self-defense classes when I moved here."

The colonel frowned. "Why didn't you join another

martial arts club? There's a jujitsu dojo just down the street."

"My foster parents aren't big on girls fighting," she explained with a sigh. "In fact, they're not big on *anything* I like doing. They're very . . . traditional in their ways."

"Would you like to start training again?"

Charley shrugged. "Sure. My dad always hoped I'd become a black belt."

"Well, you can wear any color belt you like," replied the colonel. "The style of martial arts you'd be taught isn't based on grades in the dojo; it's based on its effectiveness in the street."

He flipped open the brown folder on the table, and Charley saw a stack of papers with her name on it, along with a pile of photographs. Several were recent, including some long-distance shots of her rescuing the boy from the great white. The colonel flicked through to a section headed Education.

"I see from your school reports that you were a straight-A student until recently," he said. "Why the sudden drop-off?"

"I couldn't see the point," Charley replied with sharp honesty, shocked that the colonel had so much information on her.

Colonel Black considered this. "Loss of focus? That's understandable considering what you've been through in your life." He flipped past police reports on Kerry's abduction, news clippings of her parents' hijacked flight and confidential files regarding her fostering. "But the way you're—"

Charley slammed her hand down on the file. "How did you get all this personal stuff on me?" she demanded.

"Online research and a few connections," he replied. "But, as I was saying, the way you're going, you're headed on a self-destructive course. Charley, you need to—"

"Listen, General—"

"Colonel," he corrected her sharply.

"Sorry, *Colonel*. I really think you've got the wrong person. I'm no bodyguard. When my best friend was kidnapped, I . . ." Charley suddenly felt herself choking up. "I did nothing. I froze. I . . . failed Kerry."

"You were a defenseless little kid, Charley," said the colonel matter-of-factly. "You can't blame yourself for what happened. But now you *can* stop those things from happening to others."

Fighting back tears at the painful memory of her friend's abduction, Charley quietly asked, "How?"

"By becoming a bodyguard for other young at-risk individuals."

Charley stared through the window at the passing traffic, her mind a whirl of conflicting thoughts and emotions. She felt both thrilled and deeply uneasy at the proposal, flattered but puzzled that he'd selected her. How had this so-called colonel found her in the first place? Was he taking advantage of her vulnerable background? Was the whole thing a setup or a real opportunity?

The colonel closed the file and laid a black business card on the table. Charley glanced at the silver embossed logo of a shield with guardian wings.

"What's this?" she asked.

"Your future."

Charley eyed the single phone number running along the bottom edge.

"It's entirely up to you whether you call," said the colonel, rising to his feet. "But ask yourself this: Do you want to run scared all your life? Or do you want to take a stand and fight back?"

6

Charley felt the warm night breeze caress her as she sat on the golden sand, listening to the waves roll in. Farther down the beach a campfire flickered orange, illuminating the pack of young surfers gathered to party and surf the night away. Someone was playing an acoustic guitar and singing, *"We all need a shelter to keep us from the rain. Without love, we're just lying on the tracks waiting for a train..."*

The song's lyrics hit home hard for Charley. They seemed to sum up her situation. Without her parents, or her best friend, life felt desperately empty and without purpose. She was struggling on a daily basis to fight off depression. Only her surfing gave her a brief respite from the constant storm raging in her mind. No wonder her foster parents were giving up on her.

But was she now being offered a shelter from that storm—a chance to give her life real purpose?

The other surfers joined in the chorus and Charley recognized the song as Ash Wild's "Only Raining." Currently the most popular song in the country, possibly the entire world. The teenage rock star from Britain had taken the Billboard charts by storm.

"It's only raining on you, only raining. It's only raining on you right now, but the sun will soon shine through . . ."

Charley prayed that it would. She'd been caught in the rain for so long now that she'd forgotten what it was like for life to shine upon her. But should she take the extreme decision of joining a secret security agency? The whole concept of young bodyguards seemed not only insane but illegal. And could she trust the colonel? His recruitment methods seemed wildly unorthodox. Yet Deputy Sheriff Valdez had checked his credentials, and they'd proved to be solid.

The song came to an end, and the surfers' applause and laughter was carried to her on the breeze. It sounded distant and faint, as if from another dimension, and at that moment Charley did feel caught between two worlds—the dead-end one she was living in, and a new one that offered a whole host of possibilities. Perhaps it even offered redemption— a unique chance to atone for her failure to save her friend Kerry.

How she wished she had someone she could talk to.

Charley stared up at the heavens, awash with gleaming stars. "What should I do?" she whispered in a prayer to her parents. How she missed them—her mother's kindness and the loving way she used to brush Charley's hair before bed; her father's strength and the warm, secure embrace of his arms. She searched the constellations, wondering if her parents were somewhere up there. "Should I become a bodyguard?" she asked.

A shooting star traced a line across the sky.

Charley had her reply . . . but did it mean yes or no?

"There you are!" said a delighted voice as Bud materialized out of the darkness and plonked himself down beside her. "I was beginning to think you'd sneaked away again. What are you doing over here all alone?"

Charley offered him an apologetic shrug. "I needed some space to think."

"About what?" he asked, shifting closer.

Charley sighed and hesitated. She hardly knew Bud, but who else could she talk to? Besides, he seemed like a genuinely nice guy and had proven trustworthy by not revealing her name to the press. "Have you ever been faced with an impossible decision? One that could change your life forever?"

Bud furrowed his brow thoughtfully. "No," he admitted. "But I suppose it'd be like confronting that epic wave, the one that promises to break *so sweetly*." He pointed to the ocean, his hand rising and falling to indicate the immense size of the swell. "A legendary wave! You may never have surfed anything so huge in your life. The chances are you'll wipe out big-time. But—and here's the kicker—you *might* conquer it and ride all the way in."

He turned to Charley, his eyes gleaming with an irresistible zeal. "That wave might come only once in a lifetime, Charley. So I say, go for it!" He edged closer to her in the sand, until their knees were touching. "Now, what is this impossible decision?"

Charley was momentarily stunned by the clarity of his answer. On an impulse, she hugged him and kissed him on the cheek, then stood up and brushed the sand from her shorts.

"W-where are you going?" Bud asked, a baffled and forlorn expression on his face as she strode off up the beach.

Charley called back from the darkness, "To catch that once-in-a-lifetime wave!"

7

"I saw you stroll across the marketplace. I caught your walk but not your face," sang Ash Wild with gutsy energy into the studio mic. *"Yet what I saw in that one short glimpse is all my mind has thought of since . . ."*

Ash strummed hard on his electric guitar, a bluesy rock riff that harked back to Jimi Hendrix's "Voodoo Child." The drummer and bassist were grooving behind him, their rhythms locked in tight. The keyboard player, his head bobbing to the beat, stabbed at his Hammond organ, counterpointing Ash's driving guitar line. When the chorus kicked in, the four of them belted out in harmony, *"Beautiful from afar, but far from beautiful!"*

At its climax, Ash launched into a blistering guitar solo, his fingers ripping up the fretboard. Eyes shut tight and lower lip clamped between his teeth, he pulled every last drop of emotion from the notes he struck. Then, at the solo's peak, a string snapped.

Ash reacted in frustration by throwing his guitar to the floor, where it clanged and screamed in protest. "I was finally about to nail that solo!"

With a furious kick, he punted his soda bottle, spraying sticky liquid over everyone's gear. The drummer rolled his eyes at the bass player, who reached over and pulled the plug to the guitar amp, cutting the earsplitting feedback.

"Let's take a break," came the producer's weary voice over the studio monitors.

Ash stormed out of the studio and into the control room. The producer, a long-haired legend known as Don Sonic, was stationed at a colossal mixing desk like Sulu from *Star Trek*. He leaned back in his chair and interlocked his fingers behind his head.

"I reckon we can patch together a complete solo from the other fifty or so takes," he suggested.

"That's not good enough!" Ash muttered with a sullen shake of his head. "It'll sound false."

"To you, maybe, but not your fans. I can make it appear seamless for the record."

Ash stomped up the basement studio's stairs. "Never. We'll try it again later."

Don called after him, "You're a perfectionist, Ash. That's your gift . . . and your problem!"

"Yeah, yeah, whatever," mumbled Ash, but he knew his

producer was right. And that's what really frustrated him. He could record a song a million times, yet it never matched the ideal version in his head.

At the top of the stairs, he turned right into a sleek open-plan kitchen. An aging hulk of a man in a faded black T-shirt, its seams stretched by his bulging tattooed arms, hunched over the breakfast bar. He was idly flipping through a tabloid newspaper and sipping from a mug of black coffee.

"Hi, Big T," said Ash, acknowledging his bodyguard.

"Ash," he grunted with a nod of his bald domed head. Closing the paper, he took up a position by the patio doors, where he casually scanned the garden beyond, taking in its designer wooden decking, oval swimming pool and hot tub.

Ash appreciated Big T. The man knew when to talk and when to give him space. Opening the refrigerator door, Ash took out a fresh soda and twisted off the cap. There was a sharp hiss as the contents foamed up. Quickly putting his lips to the top, he took a long slug and closed his eyes. Ash tried to calm himself down. Just like the fizz in a soda bottle, if he got shaken up, his emotions exploded uncontrollably—often with regrettable consequences. Yet it was this same deep well of emotion that compelled him to write his songs—both a blessing and a curse, he supposed.

Wandering through to the dining room, Ash was greeted by a table overflowing with letters, packages, teddy bears and bouquets of flowers. On the far side of this mountain of mail sat a young brunette woman in a pearl-white silk blouse and pencil skirt. Her delicate chin was cupped in the palm of one hand as she skim-read a letter.

"Is this *all* for me, Zoe?" he asked, picking up an envelope with his name scrawled in red ink and dotted with glittery hearts and kisses.

"No, darling, not all of it," the publicity executive murmured, her accent polished by an English private-school education. Ash frowned in mild disappointment. Then Zoe pointed a manicured finger toward the hallway. "There're another six mailbags out there. Whoever leaked your home address on the Internet has a lot to answer for!"

Sighing, Zoe returned to sorting the piles of fan mail. Ash picked up a random letter from one of the stacks:

Dear Ash,

I'm utterly WILD for you! Ever since I was introduced to you and your music by a friend, I've followed you online, bought all your albums and supported you every step of the way. Your music has inspired me to stay true to myself and never give up on my dreams. One of my dreams is to meet you in

person. It would be amazing if I could come
backstage at one of your concerts. Would
that be possible? Please write back.

All my love,
Paige Anderson

PS: I enclose a photo so you know who I am.

Ash glanced at the picture of a grinning girl with braces on her teeth. "Is every fan letter like this?" he asked.

Tilting her head to one side, Zoe replied, "No, not all; others are *much* more obsessive than that. Certain fans write to you literally every day!"

"Like my ex-girlfriend?" suggested Ash.

"Ha-ha," said Zoe drily. "I thought you said Hanna wanted nothing to do with you."

"Yeah, but she might have changed her mind and forgiven me." He eyed a huge stack of letters on a separate table. "What's that pile?"

"Your Wildling fan club from America. Jessie Dawson, the girl who runs it, forwarded just a *small* selection so far."

As Zoe continued to sift through the various piles, Ash came across a large brown package. "Who's this from?" he asked, inspecting the address label. "There's no postmark."

Zoe glanced up and shrugged. "I haven't gotten to that one yet."

"Feels heavy," he said, weighing the package in his hands. His fingers came away slightly oily. "Smells of marzipan. I think someone sent me a cake—"

Without warning, Big T burst into the room. "Don't open that!" he yelled, grabbing the package from him. "It might be a bomb!"

8

The explosion was earsplitting. Charley sprinted around the corner of the building and was confronted by utter carnage. Shattered glass and debris were strewn across the charred ground. Her eyes stung from the acrid smoke billowing in the air. And somewhere amid the bomb-blasted wreckage a person was screaming in agony.

Charley started to dash forward but was grabbed by her arm and yanked back.

"Secondary devices!" warned Jason, glaring at her. Jason was a heavyset cinder block of a boy from Sydney and a Guardian recruit like herself.

"Of course," Charley replied. She could have kicked herself for forgetting the first rule of attending an incident: *Do not become a casualty yourself.*

In an attack of this nature, the terrorists often planted a second bomb, its purpose to kill and maim those who rushed to help the first victims. And there were numerous other hazards following an explosion: fuel leaks, chemical spillages, fires, loose masonry and exposed power lines. All risks had to be assessed before approaching a casualty.

Charley scanned the first fifteen feet ahead of her: no obvious danger. Then, together with Jason and two other guardians—David, a tall loose-limbed Ugandan boy, and José, a streetwise Mexican kid with oil-black hair—Charley performed a wider sweep of the area. They covered a sixty-foot perimeter. All this time the screaming continued, a desperate plea for help that was impossible to ignore.

"Clear!" called David as he finished the initial inspection of the bomb site.

The smoke was beginning to disperse and Charley spotted the casualty—a teenage boy. Propped against a wall, his face was caked in dust and streaked with blood.

"Over here!" she cried, racing across to him. But she stopped in her tracks when she saw the severity of the boy's injuries. Aside from the bleeding gash across his forehead, his upper left leg had suffered a major fracture. A sharp white splinter of thigh bone was sticking out at an odd angle, with tissue, muscle and white tendons all exposed. Blood was pumping from the open wound, pooling in a sticky mess on the concrete. The gruesome sight turned Charley's stomach.

"What are you waiting for?" cried Jason, pushing past her with the medical kit.

Snapped out of her daze, Charley knelt down beside the boy.

"It's okay," she told him, resting a hand gently on his shoulder. "We're going to look after you."

The boy's unfocused eyes found Charley, and he stopped screaming. "C-can't hear you!" he gasped.

Charley repeated her words, louder this time, realizing the bomb's blast had deafened him.

Jason glared at her. "Are you going to talk or act?" he muttered, opening the med-kit and tossing her a pair of latex gloves.

"I'm trying to reassure him, that's all," she shot back.

"Then do something useful," said Jason irritably.

Gloves on, Charley pressed her hands to the gaping wound. The casualty cried out in pain. "Sorry," she said with a strained smile. "I have to stem the blood loss. I'm Charley, by the way. What's your name?"

"Blake," groaned the boy. *My leg hurts!*"

"Get a tourniquet on him fast," instructed Jason.

David whipped off his belt and wrapped it around the boy's upper leg. He pulled it tight, and Charley removed her blood-soaked hands as Jason applied a dressing. With an antiseptic wipe, Charley cleaned the grime from the boy's face and inspected the gash on his forehead.

"Cut looks superficial," she told the others.

"But bruising around the area indicates a violent impact.

Possibility of concussion," corrected José, attaching a blood pressure monitor to the casualty's arm.

Charley nodded, disappointed at not assessing the injury correctly. Then she noticed the boy's eyes losing focus and his eyelids closing.

"Blake, stay with me!" He looked at her weakly. "Tell me, where are you from?"

"M-Manchester," he gasped between pained breaths.

"I've heard of Manchester. It's in the north of England, isn't it? I'm from California, so this country is still new to m—"

"Blood pressure dropping," interjected José, studying the monitor's readout. He placed two fingers against the boy's neck. "Pulse weakening."

The situation was deteriorating too fast for Charley to compute. Her brain suffered a logjam of information as all her first-aid training spewed out in one garbled mess: *Resuscitation . . . Anaphylactic shock . . . Dr. ABC . . . Hypoxia . . . Myocardial infarction . . .*

Dr. ABC was the only thing that got through the jumble. *Danger. Response. Airway. Breathing. Circulation.*

They'd already checked for danger. The casualty was responsive. And the boy's airway was clear since he could talk. He was also breathing, if a little rapidly. So it was his circulation that was the critical issue now.

"The tourniquet's on. What else can we do?" Charley asked, trying to keep the desperation out of her voice.

"He needs fluids," said José. "To replace the lost blood."

Searching through the med-kit, he pulled out a pouch of saline solution and handed Charley a cannula. "Get this in him," he said.

Charley tore off the wrapper around the sterile needle and tube. Pulling up the boy's sleeve, she hunted for a suitable vein. Her hands trembled as she held the needle over his bare skin. She'd only ever practiced inserting a cannula on a false limb during their first-aid training. In a real-life situation—under pressure—it was far more difficult.

"Let me do it!" Jason snapped.

Charley bit her tongue as he snatched the needle from her grasp. Jason always lost patience with her, and his attitude made her feel inadequate.

While Jason inserted the cannula, José kept an eye on the boy's blood pressure and David rechecked the tourniquet. This left Charley feeling like a spare wheel on the team. Not sure what else to do, she continued talking to the casualty.

"Don't worry, Blake, an ambulance is on its way," she told him. "We'll get you to a hospital in no time. You'll be fine. So tell me about Manchester—is it a nice place to visit? I've heard that . . ." Charley knew she was babbling, but the boy seemed reassured. That is, until his breathing started to accelerate abnormally. His face screwed up in agony as he fought for every breath. "What's wrong?" she asked.

"Check his chest," David suggested, his calm manner poles apart from the panic she was experiencing.

Charley lifted the boy's shirt. The whole right-hand side of his chest was bruised purple.

"Looks like a possible tension pneumothorax," said José.

"A tension *what*?" cried Charley, vaguely recalling the term but not the condition. With every passing second, she felt even more out of her depth.

"Air in his chest cavity!" exclaimed Jason as he grabbed the oxygen cylinder strapped to the side of the medical kit. "It's crushing his lungs."

He fitted a mask to the patient and began the oxygen flow to reduce the risk of hypoxia, a dangerous condition that could lead to permanent brain damage and even death.

"We'll need to perform an emergency needle decompression," said José, handing Charley a large-bore needle with a one-way valve.

Jason and David repositioned the casualty so he was lying flat. Charley stared at the disturbingly long needle. Determined not to hesitate this time, she located the second intercostal space on the boy's chest and prepared for insertion.

"NO!" cried José, grabbing her wrist. "It must go in at a ninety-degree angle or you could stab his heart."

Charley's confidence drained away. She'd almost made a

fatal error. Suddenly the boy's body fell limp and his eyes rolled back.

"He's stopped breathing!" Jason exclaimed.

David pressed a finger to the boy's carotid artery on his neck. "No pulse either."

"He's gone into cardiac arrest!" said José, taking the needle from Charley. "Assume decompression procedure complete. Begin CPR."

Jason screwed up his face at the idea. "Well, I'm not going mouth-to-mouth with him!"

"Me neither," said David.

All eyes turned to Charley.

"Fine, I'll do it," she said, shifting into position and tilting Blake's head to deliver the initial rescue breaths.

Jason raised an eyebrow at José and whispered under his breath, "Clearly she's practiced at that!"

Charley glanced up and narrowed her eyes at Jason. "What did you say?"

"Nothing," he replied. "I'll do the chest compressions."

Between them they worked at CPR, delivering thirty chest compressions to every two rescue breaths. As he pressed down on the boy's chest, Jason sang to himself, "*Ah, ah, ah, ah, stayin' alive! Stayin' alive!*"

"This is no time for singing," snapped Charley, irritated by his constant sniping.

"It's to keep . . . the correct . . . rhythm," Jason explained, pumping hard. "Saw the actor . . . Vinnie Jones . . . do this in a commercial on TV."

After two minutes of constant CPR, a dark-haired woman strode through the haze of smoke toward them.

"Ambulance is here!" she announced. "Well done. Your casualty has survived . . . Unfortunately, the other one didn't."

9

Charley exchanged confused looks with the rest of the team before turning to their Guardian close-protection instructor. "What other one?" she asked.

Jody's olive eyes turned to the area behind them and she pointed. Seeing the bewilderment on their faces, she leaped into a ditch piled with rusting tools, where a body lay partly concealed beneath a sheet of corrugated roofing. "It's the casualty who makes the least noise that should be checked first," she said.

Charley wondered how the team had missed the full-size training mannequin during their surveillance sweep. This was their first real test since arriving at Guardian Headquarters in Wales four weeks ago—and they had made a "fatal" error.

"But Blake was in need of immediate medical attention," José argued. "He was bleeding out."

"You have to resist the impulse to treat the first casualty

you encounter. If someone's screaming, you know they're alive at least," Jody explained as she climbed out of the ditch. "In an incident with multiple victims, it's crucial to perform *triage*. Assess all casualties and sort them according to the severity of their condition, using the principle of Dr. ABC as a guide: airway, breathing and circulation—in that order. Your aim should be to *do the most for the most*."

Jody paused to allow the significance of this to sink in before continuing, "That means prioritizing the most life-threatening conditions first. In this training scenario, the victim in the ditch had a blocked airway. If you'd spotted them, taken a moment to remove the obstruction, then put them in the recovery position, that person would still be alive now."

Jason scowled at Charley, and she knew she was to blame. The mannequin had been in *her* area during the initial sweep. "I suppose that means we've failed," said Jason.

Jody studied the notes on her clipboard. "Not necessarily. It's a team assessment. José, you demonstrated excellent medical knowledge and diagnosis. David, a calm and level-headed approach to an emergency. Jason, you were proactive as team leader and performed a clean insertion of the cannula. And, Charley . . ."

Charley braced herself for the worst. She knew she'd suffered a "brain freeze" and that she'd messed up the needle compression.

"Despite a rash entry into the danger zone and a potentially serious medical error, you showed good communication with the casualty and a willingness to do what was necessary. The rest of the team should take note"—she directed her gaze at Jason and David—"because one can't be self-conscious or inhibited during an emergency. If the situation demands CPR, then get on with it. Failure to act fast enough could mean the difference between life and death."

"And what about me?" asked Blake. He sat up, his fake wound still seeping blood. "I deserve an award for that acting!"

Jody arched a slim eyebrow. "Well, you certainly made more fuss than Rescue Annie over there."

"Yeah, you screamed like a girl," said Jason.

Blake shrugged it off. "Wouldn't you, with a bunch of clowns about to jab your arm and pound your chest?" He removed the cannula with José's help and pressed a Band-Aid to the resulting pinprick of blood, then glanced over at Charley. "At one point I thought you really were going to stab me with that needle!"

Charley responded with an awkward smile, embarrassed by her relative medical incompetence.

José laughed. "That certainly would have given you something to scream about."

"What? Isn't this enough?" said Blake, pointing to the gory fake wound attached to his thigh.

Jody cleared her throat to regain everyone's attention.

"Taking into account everyone's marks and considering one of the casualties died, I'm afraid the team didn't make the grade on this first-aid test. I'm recommending a reassessment in a week's time."

She ignored the team's collective groan. "You need to practice these skills until they become second nature. Remember, first aid is important in any walk of life but fundamental to being a bodyguard."

"I'd have thought our martial arts skills would be more important," mumbled Jason.

Jody glared at him. "Not necessarily. During your assignments, it's unlikely you'll ever need that high kick or spinning backfist you've practiced over and over, but you *will* need knowledge of first aid. Your Principal is far more likely to die choking on a pretzel than to be shot. In my opinion, if you're not trained in first aid, then you're not a *real* bodyguard."

10

"Martial arts are essential for a bodyguard!" stated Steve, their unarmed-combat instructor, later that afternoon. At six foot two, the ex–Special Air Service soldier was a walking mountain of muscle, and no one dared argue with him. Nor did anyone risk mentioning that Jody held a different opinion. "But, as you've discovered over the past four weeks, it isn't necessary to be the next Bruce Lee or to be able to scratch your ears with your own feet!"

The class of ten recruits chuckled at this, their laughter echoing around the spacious gymnasium. They were the first batch of trainees to be drafted into the Guardian organization, and the facilities, located in an old Victorian-era school in a remote valley of the Brecon Beacons mountain range in Wales, were a mix of run-down decay and high-tech modern. The newly equipped computerized fitness center stood in stark contrast to the cold and drafty locker rooms. But Colonel Black had promised that renovation was in progress.

The handful of recruits lined up in two rows to form a corridor down which their instructor slowly paced. Charley was at the far end opposite Blake. A cocky Mancunian with spiked black hair and a permanent grin, he was relatively friendly to her, unlike Jason. The other recruits were pleasant enough, but none had made any special effort to get to know her. Being the only girl seemed to set her apart.

"All you need is an understanding of body mechanics and a few simple techniques to preempt or disarm an attacker," Steve explained. "With these skills at your disposal, you can control people of all shapes and sizes with very little effort."

He stopped in front of Jason. Broad-chested with bulging biceps and an anvil jaw, Jason was the largest of the recruits.

"The principle is simple," said Steve, indicating for Jason to grab his T-shirt as if to assault him. "For instance, a wrist will rotate only so far. So, by manipulating it and using the attacker's own momentum to force it beyond normal movement, you can control and disable that person. Jason, take a swing at me."

Still holding his instructor's shirt, Jason clenched his right fist to let loose a roundhouse punch. As the strike arced toward him, Steve gripped Jason's left hand between his thumb and forefinger, twisting it back the other way. As he spiraled the wrist to breaking point, Jason instantly abandoned his punch and doubled over in pain. Steve followed up by firmly pushing the back of Jason's knuckles toward his elbow. With his arm locked out, Jason had no option but to drop to the floor, where he lay writhing like a speared snake.

Charley decided that was a technique she needed to learn—if only to put Jason in his place.

"If I had applied a touch more pressure, his wrist would have snapped like a twig," Steve explained matter-of-factly. "But to the casual onlooker it would appear I've done relatively little. So it maintains the principle of minimum force, which keeps me within the law. And if the attacker has a broken wrist, it's attributed to their own force when resisting, not any brutality on my part."

He released Jason, who shook the ache from his wrist and stood back in line.

"For me, this is what makes martial arts so essential for a bodyguard: the ability to control people with the illusion of minimum force."

"But what if someone has a knife?" asked Blake. "Surely we have to do more than a basic wrist lock."

"Absolutely," said Steve. "But the principle of NRP always applies. Any self-defense must be *necessary*, *reasonable* and *proportional* to the attack. So, if someone has a knife, you have every right to break that attacker's arm. However, if the potential threat is simply an overenthusiastic fan, you can't go around decking them."

"That's a shame!" Jason remarked.

Steve shot him a hard stare. "Maybe so, but we don't want

any of you appearing on a tabloid front page with your fist slamming into a fan's face while your Principal looks on in horror. Remember, you're protecting the Principal's image as well as their safety . . . *and* our organization's covert status."

He beckoned Blake to step forward.

"That's why I'm going to show you how to take down an opponent with just your fingertips."

Charley edged forward in anticipation with the rest of the recruits.

"The jugular takedown is an excellent self-defense technique," explained their instructor, "especially if the aggressor is trying to strangle you from the front."

Steve nodded to Blake to reach up and put his hands around his muscled neck in an imitation attack.

"First, locate the notch at the base of the throat, just above the collarbone," he instructed, spearing the tips of his right hand and resting his middle finger on Blake's soft depression of skin. "At the same time, slip your other hand behind the attacker's neck to gain control of their body. Finally, push in and down, *hard*, aiming toward the ground behind your attacker's feet."

Steve's move was so quick and Blake's reaction so sudden and extreme that Charley barely had time to blink before Blake was on the ground, choking and gagging. It was as if their instructor had cut the strings of a puppet.

"If necessary, you can follow up with some disabling

strikes before making your escape," Steve went on, mimicking a punch to the kidneys and groin. "I guarantee this jugular takedown will drop any individual, however big or ugly they are."

"And Blake sure is ugly!" teased Jason.

"Take a look in the mirror, dingo head," Blake rasped as Steve helped him back to his feet.

"I would, but the sight of your face already cracked it!" replied Jason, and the rest of the class broke out in laughter.

"Cut the joking!" barked Steve. "Now pair up and practice."

Charley felt like a lame duck, standing alone as the other recruits buddied up. Being the only girl, it seemed she was always the last choice, the weakest player on the team. Plus, all the other recruits had arrived with some combat training, whether it was David's military experience, José's street-fighting skills or Jason's junior championship boxing title. All she could claim were a few months of women's self-defense classes.

Blake looked at her. "Want to partner up?"

"Sure," said Charley, relieved to be asked. She noticed he was still rubbing his throat. "Are you all right?"

Blake nodded, then snaked a hand behind her neck to perform the technique on her. "I warn you—it's a shock when it happens."

"Fine, I'm read—" Blake's fingers thrust into her jugular notch and shut off her windpipe. An awful gagging sensation caused her body to fold in on itself to escape the crippling discomfort. One moment she was standing. The next she was sprawled on the floor.

"Effective, isn't it?" said Blake, offering his hand to help her up.

Charley could only nod as she fought back the desire to vomit. Now it was her turn to inflict the technique on Blake. Clasping his neck with one hand, she placed the tips of her fingers in the notch above his collarbone and pushed. Blake grimaced and gagged slightly but didn't drop to the floor. His knees didn't even buckle.

Charley frowned. What had she done wrong? Their instructor made the technique look so easy.

"In and down," Blake reminded her.

Charley nodded and tried again. This time Blake flinched violently and crumpled under her thrusting fingertips. With surprisingly little strength, she forced him all the way to the ground.

"That's . . . it!" Blake gasped, his eyes bulging in pain.

Charley smiled and let him go. The jugular takedown *was* that simple after all.

11

"Ready yourselves for the Gauntlet!" announced Steve.

With nervous reluctance, Charley joined the others at the edge of the gym as they suited themselves up in sparring gear—gloves, shin pads, mouth guards and head guards. This was the part of the lesson that she least looked forward to. While the other recruits seemed to relish the challenge of the Gauntlet, for Charley the grueling experience just emphasized how far out of her league she was. Surrounded by bigger and stronger opponents, she was like a lamb among lions.

"Ladies first," said Steve, indicating for Charley to take up position at the head of the two rows.

Charley braced herself for the walk of pain that was the Gauntlet. Its purpose was to test their developing martial arts skills in preparation for an assault in the real world. She simply had to get from one end of the gym to the other . . . in one piece.

The first time Charley had faced the Gauntlet she'd almost fled. The prospect of fighting nine adrenaline-fueled boys each in turn had been daunting to say the least. But Steve had talked her through it, offering instruction at each attack. After a month's training, though, he evidently thought it was time she walked the Gauntlet alone.

Heart thumping, Charley took her first step. The gym seemed to stretch on forever while her opponents multiplied like gremlins. Almost at once Blake grabbed the sleeve of her T-shirt. He raised a fist and Charley hesitated, her mind racing through the techniques they'd been taught.

"Thumb compression," whispered Blake, fist hovering in midair.

Grateful for his suggestion, Charley grasped his hand on her T-shirt. Catching hold of his thumb, she squeezed it as if she were gripping a pair of pliers. Blake winced as his thumb joints were compressed. He dropped to his knees in submission.

"Nice choice of technique," remarked Steve. "Subtle yet effective. But, gentlemen, don't hold back. The enemy won't."

The next recruit took their instructor at his word and launched a left hook that caught her across the jaw. Although the gloves and headguard took the sting out of it, the punch still hit hard and her head rang like a church bell, stars sparking before her eyes. As she staggered backward, a second blow struck her in the ribs, winding her. Charley instinctively curled up, shielding herself with her arms and elbows. More punches rained down.

"Come on, fight back!" urged the recruit.

Charley reeled from his attack. Her brain jarred by the first punch, she couldn't think straight.

Seeing her struggle under the onslaught, Steve called out, "Stun then run!"

A technique from a previous lesson flashed in her mind. Charley flung out her hand in a wild arc, aiming a ridge-hand strike toward the boy's neck. Steve had told them this was one of the best targets to temporarily disable or drop an opponent. A single sharp blow could cause involuntary muscle spasms and intense pain, while a powerful one focused just below the ear could result in unconsciousness through shock to the carotid artery, jugular vein or vagus nerve. It was the ideal target for a "stun then run" counterattack.

The edge of her hand impacted the boy's nerve and he lurched sideways, the blow disorienting him enough for her to get away.

But Charley had barely recovered from that attack when David rushed at her with a rubber knife. She instinctively blocked the weapon with her forearm. It was a messy defense, and if it had been a real knife, her arm would have been cut to shreds. He went for another attack. Charley lashed out and punched him in the face. He backed off.

But Charley knew that in real life she'd have been the loser.

"Don't punch—palm!" Steve instructed her. "Remember, palm strikes are just as effective as closed fists, without the risk of damaging your hand. Also the strike looks less violent in the eyes of the public. Never forget someone is always watching or filming your Principal and consequently your every move too."

Charley had just enough time to absorb this advice before she was grabbed around the throat by José. In this instance, with the jugular takedown still fresh in her mind from earlier in the lesson, Charley jabbed her fingers into José's windpipe. A sharp thrust toward his feet and he dropped to the floor like a stone.

"Excellent!" praised Steve. "That's the sort of response I'm looking for."

Charley felt a rush of accomplishment. Finally a technique that worked for her! With four down and only five to go, her confidence began to rise. But she wasn't allowed to relish the moment for long. Jason came up behind and seized her in a reverse chokehold.

"Let's see you escape this," he hissed.

Charley struggled in his grip. She knew the first thing she had to do was to twist her head in the direction of the attacker's elbow to relieve the pressure on her windpipe. But Jason was too strong. Charley couldn't breathe . . . at all!

His biceps pressing on her carotid artery, her head began buzzing. She clawed at his arm, trying to loosen his grip. She elbowed him in the stomach, but to no avail. Within seconds, all the fight went out of her and darkness seeped into her vision . . .

12

"Did you *have* to strangle Charley till she blacked out?" cried Blake.

"Steve said don't hold back," Jason replied, his tone defensive. "Anyway, it was for her own good."

"How's that?"

"If she can't fight me off, what chance does she have against a real attacker? We're not playing games here, Blake. There are no second chances. If you get it wrong on an assignment, you'll be coming home in a body bag. I mean, what was the colonel thinking when he recruited a *girl*?"

"Don't let Jody hear you say that," warned José.

"Jody's different. She's an instructor. She knows what she's doing. Charley doesn't seem to have a clue. Don't forget it was her fault we didn't spot that second casualty during the first-aid assessment. If it weren't for Charley, we'd be passing all our assessments."

"That's unfair," said Blake. "Charley did her best."

"Come on, she virtually talked you to death!" said Jason. The others laughed.

"It's important to reassure the patient," Blake replied evenly.

"Yeah, I bet you'd like Charley to *reassure* you," teased David.

"Watch your mouth!" said Blake, obviously embarrassed.

"Well, she certainly didn't hesitate to give you mouth-to-mouth!" sniggered José.

Charley had heard more than enough. Grateful as she was for Blake's defense of her dignity, she now knew the team's true opinion of her. As the boys continued with their banter in the adjacent changing room, she quietly closed her locker and headed for the door. She'd been on the fence about joining the team for dinner anyway. Now she'd lost her appetite entirely.

Escaping the old Victorian school building that housed their training facility, Charley tramped across the gravel courtyard and wandered the grounds aimlessly. She discovered an old well and perched herself on the lip, her slender legs dangling over the fathomless black hole. Tossing a stone in, she watched it tumble, then disappear. A few seconds later she heard it plop into the unseen water below.

Charley contemplated the void beneath her feet. If she'd been in this dark mood back home in America, she'd simply have gone surfing. But there were no waves within sixty miles of Guardian's remote headquarters. Here it was all sheep, craggy hills and bleak rain. She wasn't even sure if Wales had sun! The place was a far cry from the warm beaches and glistening waters of California.

Charley had hoped that Guardian would be a fresh start for her. So had her foster parents, who'd readily agreed to the colonel's proposal—sold to them as an extension of the Peace Corps. Jenny had declared that volunteer work was the best thing for a wayward teenager like Charley and had even helped pack her bags.

But after four weeks of intensive training Charley was still struggling to clear the starting line. Aside from martial arts and advanced first aid, she was required to learn about foot formations, body-cover drills, Cooper's Color Code, threat assessments, operational planning, world affairs, hostage survival and a whole raft of other security topics that left her head spinning. Then there were early-morning runs up the Welsh mountains, followed by grueling gym sessions and daily combat classes. On top of all this, she was expected to complete her normal school studies. The learning curve wasn't so much steep as vertical!

Charley realized she might have caught the once-in-a-lifetime wave, but she was already on the verge of wiping out. Jason was right: What had Colonel Black been thinking when recruiting her? And why hadn't he told her that she'd be the only girl recruit?!

Hearing the crunch of gravel, Charley glanced over her shoulder to see Jody heading her way.

"Hey, Charley," her instructor called cheerily. "Bugsy said he'd spotted you by the well. Are you okay?"

Charley shrugged. "Yeah, fine."

Jody wiped the dirt from one of the well's granite stones and sat down next to her. "You don't look fine."

Charley stared into the black abyss of the well and said nothing.

"I heard you passed out in Steve's class. You're not suffering any ill effects, are you?"

Charley shook her head.

"Then what is it? You can talk to me, you know." Her instructor's tone was soft and sympathetic. "We girls need to stick together."

After almost a minute's silence, Charley thought she might as well come out with it. There was no one else she could talk to. "I'm not cut out to be a bodyguard."

Jody blinked. "What on earth makes you say that?"

"*I'm* not saying it. The rest of the team is."

Jody frowned. "Those boys are simply intimidated by you."

Charley let out a humorless laugh. "Yeah, right. I don't see them making so many mistakes."

"Well, I do. All the time. You're barely a month into training. It's bound to feel tough."

"But everything seems to come more naturally for the boys."

"Don't you believe that!" scoffed Jody. "They're struggling just as much as you are. They simply won't admit it."

"But I don't have their advantage of size or strength. Jason's right. If I can't beat him, what chance do I have?"

"That's why you need to be in good shape and in the gym every day."

Charley made a face. "I don't want to become some butch bodyguard."

"You don't have to. Look at me." Jody spread her slim, well-toned arms and displayed her slender yet strong physique. "You can be a rose yet still have thorns. Did you know that Wing Chun—the martial arts style Steve is teaching—was developed by a woman?"

Charley shook her head.

"Well, remember that when you're training against the boys. Bodyguarding is far more about brains than brawn." She tapped a finger to her temple. "So next time fight smarter, not harder."

Jody leaned in close to ensure she had Charley's full attention. "You see, the skills required to be an effective bodyguard aren't based on gender. Whether you're a guy or a girl, you need common sense, good communication skills, awareness, self-discipline and confidence. And we girls do have advantages over the boys."

"Like what?" asked Charley.

Jody shared a conspiratorial grin. "For a start, women think differently from men. We can multitask more effectively. We're able to see and hear many separate events at once, processing them simultaneously. This means we can spot a suspect or early signs of an attack before our male counterparts do. And, if an attack does occur, your opponent certainly won't expect *you* to be a weapon!"

Charley felt a spark of hope. "So you're saying we're better at this than the boys?"

"I'd like to think so." Jody smiled. "Female intuition and the element of surprise give us the upper hand. But if I've learned one thing in my career, it's that actions speak louder than words. Remember, we're both women in a man's world. This role isn't for the fainthearted. You need guts. You have to stand your ground with the boys. It's a matter of pride for them, so they'll do whatever's necessary to keep a girl from showing them up. But prove yourself, and you'll earn their respect."

13

The scissors cut around Ash's head with absolute precision, each snip shearing away another piece to free the idol's photograph from the magazine article. The blades sliced between the gaps of his perfectly coiffured brown hair, around the diamond-studded left ear and along the sleek curve of his jawline to the dimpled chin. His dark hazel eyes smoldered, and his upturned mouth revealed flawless teeth that gleamed like a toothpaste commercial, while the surrounding skin appeared tanned, smooth and blemish-free.

Photoshopped or not, Ash was blessed with the face of a Greek god—the perfect teen heartthrob. No wonder his posters graced the walls of millions of girls' bedrooms around the world.

With a final snip, the blades cut across the rock star's throat and the magazine dropped away.

The scissors were set aside and the cutout was carefully laid on the table, making sure not to crease it. Then some glue was applied to the back and Ash's disembodied head pasted on to a large sheet of pink paper. More glue was dabbed randomly across the collage before glitter dust and stars were sprinkled liberally over the young icon.

In the dim light of the bedside lamp—the curtains of the room still drawn despite it being midafternoon—the image now sparkled and glistened like a diamond. The love letter to the famous rock star was beginning to take shape. It just needed one final embellishment.

After the glue and glitter had been put away, a small bowl and paintbrush were placed on the table. The contents of the bowl were slowly stirred with the narrow tip of the brush until the red viscous liquid evened out. It had been a grim and sticky job to collect the blood. The piglet had squealed loudly when the butcher's knife had sliced its carotid artery. There'd been so much blood for such a small creature.

But the piglet hadn't died in vain.

Wiping the excess blood from the brush tip against the bowl's edge, a latex-gloved hand held the letter down. With childlike concentration, three words were scrawled across Ash's perfect face:

NO MORE ENCORES!

14

"A crowd is one of the most risky environments you and your Principal will face on a regular basis," Colonel Black said, his weathered hands gripping the lectern in Guardian's state-of-the-art briefing room, which doubled as a classroom. On the main wall hung a giant widescreen display onto which the colonel wirelessly cast a video of a throng of people pushing against a barrier. "In these situations you'll need to constantly scan the area and assess any possible threats."

Charley listened intently as she sat in one of the sleek high-backed lecture chairs, the furniture so new that the protective plastic film had yet to be removed from the chrome fittings. Although the outer shell remained a nineteenth-century school building, internally Guardian HQ was being revamped with the most advanced electronic hardware and equipment available. Charley and the rest of the team were also equipped with the latest tablet computers on which to take class notes and do their homework.

"So, when vetting a crowd, first try to establish brief eye contact with any suspects." The colonel thumbed the remote in his hand and the bullet points to his lecture flashed up one by one on the overhead display. "What are their eyes saying? Are they appearing shifty? Nervous? Upset? Are they fixated on your Principal or perhaps another target?"

Charley rapidly keyed the main points on her tablet, aware she was the only one taking detailed notes. But that didn't bother her. Since her chat with Jody two weeks earlier, Charley had committed herself to becoming the best bodyguard on the team. She'd spent night after night rereading the first-aid manual before her team's reassessment. And this time she hadn't suffered a logjam of information. In fact, Jody had passed her with flying colors.

Charley also exercised longer in the gym than the others, her efforts already paying off as she began to overtake the boys on their early-morning runs, her long legs and light build allowing her to bound over the rugged landscape, leaving the heftier recruits behind. And, taking Jody's advice to fight smarter, not harder, she'd persuaded Steve to give her extra martial arts training during the lunch periods, concentrating on techniques suited to her build and abilities so her combat skills would match the boys'.

This wasn't done to earn the boys' respect but to prove that a girl could do the job just as well—and that *this* girl could do it better. She owed it to her parents to be the best. And she owed it to Kerry not to give up.

"Next, look at people's hands," said Colonel Black, raising his own and revealing the remote. "What are they holding? Is one of their hands clasped around something? Or are their hands in their pockets? Or behind their back?"

He pointed to David's backpack at his feet. "Ask yourself: what's in the bag they're carrying? What about the contents of their pockets? And, finally, their clothes: are they wearing anything unusual? A bulky coat on a hot day? A hat or dark glasses to conceal their identity? All these questions should go through your head subconsciously as you assess each individual in the crowd. With practice, the process should take a matter of seconds per person."

Blake leaned across to Charley and whispered, "Can I borrow your notes after the lesson?"

Charley could tell from his roguish grin he was turning on the charm, but she didn't really mind. Blake was the only member of the team willing to fight in her corner, and she had no intention of isolating herself further. "Sure," she said.

"Thanks, you're a lifesaver," he replied with a wink.

"Pay attention, you two!" said the colonel, snapping his

fingers. "You mustn't forget a crowd is a dynamic situation. Once you've decided an individual isn't a threat, *don't* dismiss them entirely. The attacker could be a professional assassin or simply very good at hiding their intentions."

Triggering the remote, he launched an old grainy video clip of a group of men leaving a hotel and crossing the pavement to a waiting limo.

"The attempted assassination of US President Ronald Reagan in 1981 demonstrates this clearly." Colonel Black pointed to a suited man walking toward the camera. "See here! This Secret Service agent looks directly at the attacker, who's offscreen. The agent doesn't consider him a threat, so ignores him and turns inward to where Ronald Reagan is about to enter his vehicle. He now has his back to the attacker."

Charley's eyes were locked on the screen as the video footage showed several gunshots going off and people diving to the ground in panic. Then President Reagan was bundled into the limo as one brave Secret Service agent spread his arms and shielded him from the deadly hail of bullets. A round caught the agent in the gut and sent him tumbling to the sidewalk, but by then Reagan was speeding safely away and the attacker was neutralized.

When the video clip finished, silence filled the room. For the first time, the young bodyguards were confronted with the brutal reality of what it meant to stand in the line of fire to protect another.

Charley raised a tentative hand. "Did the agent who was shot *die*?"

Colonel Black shook his head. "No, he made a full recovery. But no one need have been hurt if that first agent had done his job properly and not turned his back on the crowd. Don't make that mistake yourself."

He switched off the overhead display. "Now let's put these skills into practice. José, you're a famous film star."

"Naturally," he replied, getting to his feet with a swagger.

"Yeah, a stand-in for baby Groot!" quipped Jason.

"Ha-ha, that's very funny for someone who looks like Skippy the Kangaroo!" José shot back.

Colonel Black silenced the pair with a sharp look before continuing his briefing. "Unfortunately, José, your last film offended a few people and you're the target for a potential attack. Jason, you'll be his bodyguard. Blake, David and Charley, you'll form the Personal Escort Section, or PES team, as we like to call it." He opened a door leading through to an adjacent classroom. "Now, go and meet your fans!"

Leaping from their seats, the PES team hurriedly positioned themselves into a protective arrowhead formation around their Principal, as they'd been taught to do by the colonel in a previous lesson. Then they entered the room to be greeted by a small crowd of the other five recruits and instructors impersonating excited fans.

"Hey, José, can I have your autograph?" asked one boy.

"Absolutely, my friend," grinned José, playacting his superstar role to the max. "Any more takers?"

The mini-crowd surged forward and surrounded him. Charley and the rest of the team struggled to keep them at a safe distance as José signed more autographs and posed for selfies. All the while Charley's eyes darted from each person's face to their hands to their clothes. She hunted for signs of a would-be attacker.

Of course, there might not be one. During their training, they'd enacted numerous different scenarios. Sometimes there was an attack. Other times nothing happened. Just as in real life.

But on this occasion Charley noticed their surveillance tutor Bugsy hanging at the back of the crowd. He was making no effort to meet José the film star, and this unnatural behavior set him apart from the others.

Suddenly they heard wild shouting. Jason and the rest of the PES team spun toward the disruption. The room's widescreen display had been switched on and was blaring out a newsreel of a riot. With the Guardian recruits distracted, Bugsy pushed through the crowd and swung a bottle at José's head.

No one on the team reacted to the attack . . . apart from Charley.

Having kept one eye on her suspect, she was ready for the surprise assault. She leaped to José's defense, shoving him aside and shielding him with her body, only for the bottle to strike her instead. It smashed to pieces over her head, and she staggered under the impact.

Everyone in the room froze.

"Was that a *real* bottle?" asked Jason, more in awe at the idea than out of any concern for Charley.

"No. It's just sugar glass," replied Bugsy in a matter-of-fact tone.

"Well, it hurt like one!" cried Charley. She took her hands away. There was no blood, but she could feel a mighty bruise forming. "Couldn't you have used a plastic one?"

"Wouldn't be realistic enough," Bugsy explained. "You have to be able to take a hit as a bodyguard—and still function." He eyed the other members of the team. "Which is the reason I'm wondering why the rest of you haven't evacuated your Principal yet!"

Snapped from their daze, Jason and the others grabbed José and rushed him out. Charley, still reeling from the blow, stumbled after them back into the briefing room.

With the exercise over, José stopped acting the film star as Blake helped Charley to a chair. "Thanks for taking the hit for me," said José.

"My pleasure," Charley groaned, cradling her head in her hands.

"That looked like it really hurt!" remarked Blake as he knelt down beside her.

Charley gave another groan in reply.

Jason grinned. "She should have blocked it properly."

"Well, I didn't see *you* react," the colonel pointed out. "And you were José's bodyguard!"

The smug grin fell from Jason's face as he was shamed into silence.

The colonel nodded at Charley. "At least someone was paying attention in my class. You might be hurting, Charley, but you've learned a valuable lesson—always expect the unexpected."

15

"Colonel, do you have a minute?" asked Charley, racing after him as he headed for his Range Rover in the Guardian HQ parking lot. She'd tried to pin the colonel down on numerous occasions, but, apart from his specialty classes, he was rarely around, always rushing off on urgent business-related matters.

The colonel stopped, his highly polished boots scrunching on the gravel of the school courtyard. "Of course, Charley. How's your head?"

"Okay, I guess," she replied, tenderly testing the growing bruise with a finger.

"It's a hard lesson. But one you won't forget."

Charley nodded and winced as her skull gave a throb. "Colonel, you said to expect the unexpected, but I didn't expect to be the only girl at Guardian. If you believe girls make good bodyguards, why haven't you recruited more?"

The colonel's expression remained impassive. "You were

the first I'd found up to the task . . . and the only one since to say yes."

Charley was taken aback to discover this. "But why didn't you tell me?"

"Would it have made a difference to your decision?"

Charley shrugged. "Probably not. But it'd be nice to have the company. I feel a bit outnumbered by the boys."

"Don't worry, I'm working on it," he said with a wry smile. "Just takes time to find suitable recruits."

"So, how *do* you find recruits?" she asked. The question had been bugging her for a while.

"They usually make themselves known to us—through their actions."

"Like when I saved that boy from the shark?"

The colonel nodded. "I was actually on vacation," he admitted. "But your heroics caught my eye. And after our little chat in the dunes and subsequent research, I saw real potential in you." He placed a hand on her shoulder and looked her in the eye. "Listen, I know from Jody you've been questioning your abilities. *Don't.* You're doing well. Just keep your chin up."

He gave her shoulder a squeeze, then pulled out his car keys. The Range Rover beeped, its parking lights flashing. He opened the driver's-side door and got in. "And my advice for handling the boys: give as good as you get."

Gunning the engine, Colonel Black saluted a good-bye,

then sped off down the long driveway, the Range Rover's heavy-duty tires kicking up gravel as they went.

Charley stood in the courtyard, mulling over his words, until the car had crested the hill. Colonel Black clearly believed in her. Her efforts *were* being recognized—if not by the team, then at least by those who counted.

With a more confident spring in her step, Charley headed back inside the school building. She found Blake sitting at the bottom of the staircase in the entrance hall.

"What are you doing?" she asked.

"Waiting for you," he replied with a warm smile.

Charley blinked in shock. Then she remembered. "Ah, yes. You wanted my class notes," she said, pulling out her tablet from her bag. "I could've just emailed them to you."

"I know," he said, his eyes lingering on her. "But it's nicer to do things personally."

Charley felt a warmth in her cheeks. Before Blake could notice the effect his gaze was having on her, she busied herself transferring the notes to his tablet. "There you go," she said.

Blake smiled again. "Thanks. I really appreciate it. I tend to miss things—I'm not as fast as you at typing."

"No problem. Anytime," she replied breezily, returning the tablet to her bag.

Blake stood up, closer to her than she expected, and was about to say something else when they were interrupted.

"Hey, Blake!" called David, appearing in the hallway. "Are you coming to play soccer or not?"

"Yeah," he replied, then turned back to Charley. "Catch you later?"

Charley nodded and watched him run off to join the others. As she made her way upstairs to her room, she couldn't shake the smile from her face. Perhaps there were advantages to being the only girl.

16

"What's this?" said Bugsy, pointing to a blue Tupperware box on the desk.

Charley and the rest of the team exchanged bemused glances. The answer seemed obvious. "A lunch box," said Blake.

"No. It's a bomb."

Everyone instinctively flinched away, the briefing room suddenly feeling too small.

"A real one?" José queried.

Their surveillance tutor gave a nod of his bald head and grinned as deviously as the Cheshire cat from *Alice in Wonderland*. "This one happens to be a smoke bomb," he revealed, removing the lid and exposing the small package of wires and components inside. "But it'd be a simple matter to upgrade this to a fire bomb or a high-explosive device capable of destroying this entire building."

He held up a red block of what appeared to be Play-Doh.

"PBX," said Bugsy. "Plastic-bonded explosive."

He tossed it to Jason, who caught it, freaked out and almost dropped the innocuous-looking block on the floor.

"Relax, Jason, PBX requires a considerable shock to set it off."

"Better not look at it then," warned Charley. "You might trigger an explosion."

The class burst into laughter and Jason scowled. José raised a hand to high-five her. "Harsh but fair, girl!"

Claiming the high five, Charley realized, for the first time, she was making ground with the team. As the colonel said, she just had to give as good as she got.

"Eat PBX!" Jason growled, lobbing the explosive at her.

She caught it in one hand, much to his annoyance. The PBX was surprisingly light, pliable and slightly greasy to the touch.

"You still have to pay it respect, though," said Bugsy as Charley tested the material with a squeeze. "What you're holding in your hand would be enough to kill everyone in this room."

Charley stared in horror at the deadly block, then hurriedly passed it back to her tutor.

"Pound for pound, PBX packs a pretty big punch. So what's the main advantage of a bomb over other weapons?" he asked the class.

Jason opened his mouth to reply, but Charley cut in, "The bomber doesn't have to be there."

"Exactly," said Bugsy as Jason glowered at her and slumped back in his seat. "They could be thousands of miles away and detonate it remotely with a cell phone or by fitting a timer. Compare that to using a knife or a gun, where the perpetrator has to be present and their chances of being captured or killed increase dramatically. And acquiring a gun in countries like the UK can be a serious challenge. However, with a few easily obtainable household items, any schoolboy can make a bomb."

"Cool!" said José, sitting up in his chair with interest. "Are you going to show us how?"

"Absolutely not, but I'll teach you what to do if you spot one," replied Bugsy as the first slide of his presentation appeared on the widescreen display. "The rule of the Four Cs: *confirm, clear, cordon, control.*"

Charley picked up her tablet and began to input the meaning of the Four Cs into her class notes. Blake smiled at her and winked, confident he could rely on her notes. Charley smiled back.

"A bomb can be hidden in a suspect car or truck, dropped in a garbage can or left at the roadside. It can be disguised as a backpack, a trash bag or even a cell phone. Whatever it is that arouses your suspicions, first you must *confirm* those suspicions."

"Isn't that going to be dangerous?" asked David, his question more a statement of fact than a matter of concern. To

Charley, David appeared a strong, silent type. She knew little of his past, but he always acted in the same calm and unhurried manner, whether chilling out in the common room or under fire during a training scenario. It was as if he'd seen it all before, or had seen a great deal worse in his life and was numb to it.

"Well, it certainly doesn't mean giving the suspect bag a kick, let alone opening it!" Bugsy replied. "Any suspect items must be considered booby-trapped. So, for starters, switch off any cell phones."

"But that would prevent us from calling the authorities," Blake pointed out.

"True, but radio waves are often used to trigger remote-control bombs. You don't want to accidentally set it off yourself!" Bugsy explained. "Next, establish who the item belongs to. If you can't find the owner, then the item is a threat. Whether your Principal is the intended target or not makes no difference. Bombs are indiscriminate killers."

"So if we believe it's a bomb, we *clear* the area?" asked Charley, looking up from her notes.

"Absolutely." Bugsy nodded. "Trust your gut instinct and clear to a safe distance, quickly and without panic. In Hollywood movies, you see the hero outrunning an explosion. In reality no one can outrun an explosion. One second everything is normal, and the next second everything is destroyed. The biggest killer can be the blast wave and what's contained in it—shards of glass and debris—so you need to reach a sheltered location."

"What about the other two Cs?" asked David.

"Once clear, you can call the emergency services and hand over responsibility for them to *cordon* off the area and *control* the situation. Even if the suspect item turns out to be harmless, it's better to make sure your Principal is safe than risk being blown to bits!"

Bugsy picked up a brown padded envelope from the desk and waved it in the air.

"Don't forget your friendly mailman or courier," he said with a grim expression. "Letter and parcel bombs are a favored device for terrorists, criminals and those with a grudge. Traditionally explosive or incendiary, nowadays they can be chemical, biological or even radiological."

"A nuclear letter!" José grimaced. "I'm not handling anyone's mail."

"Wise decision," agreed Bugsy. "Any attempt to open one might set it off. But as a bodyguard, you're responsible for all aspects of your Principal's safety. There are a number of telltale signs to look out for—the Seven Ss, to be exact."

On the display, the presentation bullet-pointed *Size*, *Shape*, *Sender*, *Stamp*, *Seal*, *Stain* and *Smell*.

"*Size*," began Bugsy. "The letter needs to be big enough to house the components, so will be at least five millimeters thick, and weigh over fifty grams, and may feel unusually heavy for its size. *Shape*—the package could be lopsided or lumpy, indicating possible batteries or switching systems. *Sender*—check the postmark. Where did it come from? Is the origin unusual? Is there a return address and can it be verified? *Stamp*—is there one? Or was it hand-delivered? There may even be extra postage since the last thing the perpetrator wants is his letter bomb to be returned to sender!"

The class chuckled at their tutor's black humor. Meanwhile, Charley's fingers flew across her tablet screen as she raced to take down the details. Swamped by so much information, the rest of the team had given up taking notes altogether. Charley was aware that Blake shared her notes with the others and that the boys had started relying on her to write up their lessons for future studying. Though this irritated her, she hoped it might raise her value within the team, so she let it ride. Besides, she enjoyed her regular meetings with Blake after class, and they were becoming close friends.

"*Seal*—one end may have been purposefully secured to force entry at the other end," continued Bugsy. "Also look out for a pin-sized hole indicating the use of an external arming device. *Stain*—some explosives can weep an oily residue that will produce marks on the outside of the envelope. Finally, *smell*—if there's a strange aroma of almonds or marzipan, this could indicate nitroglycerin. Then again—" Bugsy switched the presentation to a picture of a chocolate sponge cake lit by candles—"it could just be a cake!"

17

The screaming never ceased. A constant white noise of high-pitched delirium, it assaulted Ash's hotel room day and night. He unthinkingly wandered too close to a window and the screaming intensified as his name was chanted to the skies. *ASH WILD! ASH WILD!* It was so loud at one point that the glass actually vibrated in its frame.

Glancing down at the hordes of fans on the street below, Ash gave a dutiful wave. This whipped the fans into an even greater frenzy, and the street turned into a seething mass of hysterical girls. Some had been camping there for days, desperate for a glimpse of their idol following the online leak of his hotel location in London. During his initial rush of fame Ash had found their presence flattering, even reassuring. Now the permanent border guard of fans wherever he went had become claustrophobic. He felt like a goldfish trapped in a bowl, a thousand eyes watching his every movement.

Ash went back to pacing the room. The lounge area was

exactly twenty-five strides long and fourteen wide. The dimensions hadn't changed during his entire time holed up in his luxury suite, and he knew they never would. Slumping onto a plush velvet sofa, Ash picked up his acoustic guitar and began to strum.

"You lift me up," he sang softly to himself, *"because . . ."*

The lyric hung in the air, unfinished. He sought inspiration, but none came. Sighing, he tried again, repeating the phrase over and over, each time hoping to find the elusive line that would lead to the next part of the melody.

But after countless attempts he gave up. His creativity was stifled in this hotel room. He'd been cooped up far too long—at least he hoped that was the reason. Deep down he feared his muse had abandoned him altogether following the shock of the letter bomb.

How could anyone send him a lethal package like that? What had he done for anyone to hate him so much? His worst crime in his life so far had been to cheat on Hanna. But ex-girlfriends don't send letter bombs simply for kissing another girl . . . not unless they're totally crazy!

Letting the guitar slide to the floor, Ash reached for the remote and surrendered himself to daytime TV. Halfway through a repeat episode of *The Big Bang Theory*, there was a knock at the door. Ash switched the TV off. The door opened, and Big T's face with its heavy jowls and wide boxer nose appeared.

"Ms. Gibson's 'ere," he grunted in his hard Cockney accent. He stepped aside to allow Ash's manager into the room. Then, nodding politely to them both, he closed the door and resumed his guard duty outside in the hallway.

Kay Gibson greeted Ash with her arms wide. "How's my superstar?"

She strode over to him, the high heels of her Jimmy Choo shoes leaving deep impressions in the carpet. At almost six feet with chopped dyed-red hair, ruby lips and a cosmetically youthful face, Kay Gibson was a daunting bombshell of a woman. Record company executives admired her striking looks as much as they feared her brutal negotiation tactics and sharp business acumen. Within the music industry, she was known as the Red Devil or the Ruby Angel, depending on which side of the table one sat, for Kay was deeply loyal and protective of her artists and always struck the best deal for them.

"Glad to see you're not wasting your free time," she remarked, eyeing the TV remote in his hand.

Ash sighed. "I need to get out of here."

"Soon."

"That's what you always say. I've been living in this hotel room for almost two months!"

Kay gazed around at the fine furnishings, four-poster bed and original artwork lining the walls. "You don't have any complaints about the room, do you?"

"No, it's just that I'd like to be in my own place again," he explained, pulling himself into a sitting position. "I can't write here."

Kay raised a manicured eyebrow in alarm. "That's not good. But I've told you—it isn't easy acquiring new property in London. Especially one that's exclusive and secure enough to meet your needs, but . . ." Her green eyes twinkled with promise. "I'm pleased to say I've found you one at last."

Ash stared at her in disbelief. "Really? So when do I move in?"

"With any luck, by the weekend."

Ash leaped off the sofa, whooping with delight.

"But we need to tighten your security arrangements," she warned. "We don't want your new address being revealed. Just because that letter bomb turned out to be a fake doesn't mean we shouldn't take any threat seriously."

The mention of the bomb punctured Ash's buoyant mood. "Have the police found out who sent it yet?" he asked.

Kay shook her head. "They still have no leads. The only fingerprints on the packaging were yours and Big T's. The police conclude it was a well-planned hoax."

"Is their investigation over then?"

Kay nodded. "I'm afraid so. With no postmark or any other clues, they say there's nothing they can do."

"But it wasn't exactly standard hate mail, was it?"

Kay put a motherly arm around him. "It's a one-off. Think

of it as a status symbol. It means you're officially famous now."

"Wow, that's reassuring," muttered Ash.

"Don't get down about it. All the great artists receive death threats and acquire their own stalkers. Madonna. Lennon. Beyoncé—"

"But wasn't John Lennon killed by his stalker?" interrupted Ash.

Kay looked pained. "Bad example. But you don't have to worry—you've got Big T as your bodyguard. And considering what's happened, I've employed him full-time now. He's worth his weight in gold. Not literally, of course; that would cost us a small fortune." She laughed at her own joke, then became serious again. "But if that had been a real bomb, Big T would have saved your life."

Ash fell silent, his brush with death a chilling thought.

"I have something that'll put a smile back on your face," said his manager, fishing into the pocket of her tailored suit. "The master of your new single!"

She produced a flash drive. Grinning, Ash took it from her and plugged it into the portable recording studio set up in the corner of the room. He'd been waiting for his producer to put the final touches on the recording. Switching on the monitors, he loaded the file labeled *Indestructible* into his computer's media player. A driving beat in the vein of Michael Jackson's "Billie Jean" pulsed from the speakers.

A throbbing bass line amplified the groove, then a guitar riff kicked in as Ash launched into the opening verse.

"This song is going to make you a megastar like no other!" declared Kay, tapping her foot to the beat.

As the song hit the chorus, Ash's cell phone beeped. He glanced at the screen and frowned.

"What's the matter?" asked Kay.

Ash showed her the text he'd received:

Play it backward.

"Who's it from?" she asked, equally perplexed.

"Don't know," he replied. "No Caller ID."

Curiosity getting the better of him, Ash opened the file in Pro Tools and played it in reverse. The song sounded warped and alien, the words as distorted and unsettling as a satanic chant. But the message was clear enough: *"Asssshhhhh willlll dieeeee . . . Asssshhhhh willlll dieeeee . . . Asssshhhhh willlll dieeeee . . ."*

18

Clouds streaked across the gray-blue sky, their shadows chasing them over the peaks and troughs of the mountainous terrain that surrounded Guardian HQ. Shafts of sunlight speared the summits before sweeping across valleys of lush green fields speckled white with sheep. The blustery air was crisp, cool and clean to breathe—unlike the smog-tainted atmosphere of the California coast.

After almost three months, Charley was starting to appreciate the stark beauty of the Brecon Beacons. From her bench in the old school's gazebo, she could see the sweeping expanse of craggy mountains and even glimpse the impressive peak of Pen y Fan in the far distance. However, as awe-inspiring as the view was, she could never call it home. The place was just too darn cold, even with summer approaching.

Pulling her sweater around her shoulders, Charley

settled back to studying her notes. The wooden summer-house with its roof overrun by creeper vines was her secret haven—a retreat from the hectic hothouse of bodyguard training. As she read up on Bugsy's anti-surveillance tactics, she was vaguely aware of the fervent yells and cries of the other recruits playing soccer. There was a loud cheer, and she guessed one of the boys had scored a goal.

A ball rolled past the summerhouse, followed a moment later by the lithe figure of Blake jogging after it. He kicked the ball back to his teammates before noticing Charley.

"Hey," said Blake, poking his head in.

"Hey yourself," she replied, glancing up as if she hadn't seen him until then. Although they'd been spending more and more time together, she was trying not to appear needy or desperate for his company.

"What are you doing in here?" he asked.

"Reading."

Blake spied the tablet in her hands. "Charley, it's Sunday! Our *only* day off."

Charley shrugged. "What else do you suggest I do? Everyone else is playing soccer."

A twinge of guilt flashed across Blake's face. "Sorry, but I didn't think you'd be interested."

"I'm not," she replied. *But it would have been nice to be asked*, she thought.

Blake hesitated at the door, clearly questioning whether to stay or not. Then he called to the others, "Play on without me. I'm taking a break."

He sat next to her on the bench. "So, what does interest you?" he asked.

Charley stared resolutely at her notes. "Surfing."

"I didn't know you surfed," said Blake, surprised.

Charley looked sideways at him. "There're a lot of things you don't know about me."

Blake flinched at the harshness in her tone. Charley didn't know why she was being so rough on him. After all, he was the one who took her side and was pretty much her only friend among the recruits.

"I'm sorry," she mumbled. "I'm a bit fed up, that's all."

"About what?"

Charley sighed. "We've completed three months of training. I'm working as hard as everyone else, if not harder, yet I still don't feel like a full member of the team."

"Of course you are," said Blake.

Charley raised a dubious eyebrow. "You all treat me as some sort of secretary rather than a serious recruit."

"I certainly don't," Blake replied, his tone earnest. He slid closer, his leg now touching hers. "I mean, I appreciate you sharing your notes and all, but I respect you and your abilities."

"Thanks. I'm not sure the others do."

"Listen," said Blake. "It isn't easy being the only girl among a bunch of meatheads, but don't let them get to you." He glanced toward the open door, then back at her. "I like you," he admitted with a disarming smile. "A lot. And I hate to see you upset and lonely. Not when there's no need to be."

He shifted nearer. Charley could see the intention in his eyes. Briefly she considered resisting. But Blake being nice to her meant a lot in the circumstances. And as he put an arm around her shoulders, she could feel her defenses weakening. She wanted to be accepted, to be liked.

Charley closed her eyes and parted her lips . . . but pulled away at the last second.

"What's the matter?" Blake asked.

Charley looked at the door. "Didn't you hear something?"

Blake listened. Everything was quiet outside. He shook his head. Smiling, he went back in for the kiss.

This time Charley didn't pull away.

Just as their lips touched, an object clattered onto the wooden floor at their feet. It exploded, and the summerhouse billowed with smoke. Within seconds the two of them were enveloped in an impenetrable cloud. Coughing and spluttering, they staggered out into the fresh air.

Jason and the other recruits stood outside, killing themselves with laughter.

"What was *that*?" Blake exclaimed, tears streaming from his red eyes.

Jason laughed. "Bugsy's smoke bomb!"

"It looked like things were getting a little hot in there," sniggered David.

"*What is it with you?*" Charley cried, striding up to Jason, her pent-up fury with him spilling over.

"Calm down, Charley. It was just a joke," he replied, holding up his hands and backing away. "The Four Cs!"

Charley glared at him, frowning in confusion.

"We *confirmed* the threat: Blake." Jason grinned at his spluttering friend. "We *cleared* the danger zone. Now I'm afraid we'll have to *cordon* off this summerhouse and *control* you two in the future!"

Charley's face reddened. With the boys' laughter ringing in her ears and smoke still billowing from the summer house, she stormed off to her room.

19

Charley grabbed her duffel bag from under her bed and began shoving her clothes into it. Her cheeks were still burning with shame and her eyes were tearful from the acrid smoke. She felt not only humiliated by the boys' prank but also angry with herself for her moment of weakness. Labeled as Blake's *girlfriend*, she'd never be accepted as a serious member of the team now.

While she'd made some headway in gaining their respect, she knew they still considered her the token female. Charley was equally frustrated with being the only girl on the team. Where were the others the colonel had promised to recruit? After months of persistent teasing, sexist comments and snide remarks about her abilities as a bodyguard, she'd hit her limit.

Having emptied the contents of her drawers into the bag, she then picked up the picture of her parents from the bedside table. The photo had been taken the day she'd won her first surfing trophy, and the memory was still precious. It had been a perfect day, the sky cloudless, the sun glinting off the glassy waters, the waves curling like massive scoops of ice cream. She'd surfed her heart out and blown the rest of the competition out of the water. She could recall her parents' sheer joy at her achievement. They'd seen it as a milestone in her recovery from Kerry's abduction. And looking now at the proud smiles on their faces, Charley sat down and questioned what she was doing. *Am I really going to give up that easily? Let those boys get to me that much? Let them win?*

She remembered her mother once saying, "When you doubt your power, you give power to your doubt." And that was exactly what she was doing now.

There was a knock at her door. She glanced up to see Blake standing in the doorway.

"You're not leaving, are you?" he asked, his gaze flicking to her half-packed duffel bag.

"It had crossed my mind," she replied.

"Come on—it was just a stupid prank," he said, sitting next to her on the bed.

"I know that," said Charley. "But I've had enough of being the butt of all the team's jokes."

Blake sighed. "They don't mean it personally."

"Well, it feels personal to me," she replied. "Jason, especially."

"He's just jealous," said Blake, taking her hand.

"Of us?"

Blake laughed. "No, of your abilities. I know it riles him every time you outshine him in class. He simply can't accept that a girl can be better than him."

"Well, he'd better get used to it," said Charley, returning her parents' picture to the bedside table. "Because I'm here to stay."

"That's the spirit," said Blake, squeezing her hand affectionately. "Now, look, the whole team knows we like each other. So why hide it? Why not just make it official?"

Charley looked at him. It would be so easy to say yes . . . but she wanted to be accepted by the team on her own merits. Not as the *girlfriend*.

"I'll think about it," she replied. *But first I have a point to prove.*

20

"No sparring gear!" declared Steve to everyone's astonishment. "This final Gauntlet will be a real-life scenario."

A rush of adrenaline coursed through Charley's veins and her pulse raced. The recruits had been preparing themselves for this unarmed combat assessment for the past week, but none had expected to fight without protection.

Steve chortled at the shocked expressions on his students' faces. "On an assignment, you won't have the luxury of pads and headgear, nor will your attacker be wearing boxing gloves. They'll hit hard and without mercy. So get used to it. You've completed basic training—now let's see which of you makes the grade."

Steve approached Charley. "First or last?"

Holding her nerves in check, Charley replied without hesitation, "First."

She'd trained hard in the gym every day and was at the peak of physical fitness. The weeks of extra combat classes had honed her martial arts skills. If there was ever a time to prove herself as a bodyguard, once and for all, this was it.

"Remember, in a conflict you only get out what you put in," Steve advised. "Speed and aggression will always win, even if your technique is less than perfect. But perfect technique delivered with speed and aggression is *unbeatable*."

Charley took her place at the head of the Gauntlet. The other recruits were limbering up, and Jason stood at the far end, cracking his knuckles in anticipation, his eyes narrowed in an obvious challenge. Ignoring him, Charley bounced lightly on the balls of her feet and shook the tension from her arms. It was time to teach these boys a lesson.

Yet Charley was strongly aware that the odds of surviving nine consecutive attacks were slim to say the least.

"Begin!" barked Steve.

With a last deep breath, Charley headed into the Gauntlet.

The first recruit seized her wrist as if to drag her away. Charley spun her arm in a high arc, spiraling her attacker's own arm until the joints locked and pain forced him to let go. Gripping the boy's hand, she then compressed the wrist joint and forced her attacker to the ground. To ensure he didn't get up again, Charley delivered a swift kick to his gut, leaving the boy winded and wheezing on the floor.

Blake was up next. He swung a roundhouse punch at her, telegraphing it early to give her a chance to react. As much as she liked him, how she wished he *wouldn't* keep making allowances for her. In the beginning, his gestures were appreciated, but now they felt belittling, as if Blake believed she wasn't capable of defending herself against a real attack. She blocked it hard, striking at an inner nerve in his biceps muscle so that his arm became temporarily paralyzed. As the pain registered, she delivered a one-inch push to his chest. Steve had yet to teach this technique to the other recruits, so it came as a complete surprise to Blake. Like a coiled-up spring, Charley drove her palm into his solar plexus and shoved him backward. The super-powered push sent Blake flying. He landed in a heap on the floor, utterly incapacitated and fighting for breath.

The other boys immediately upped their game. The next recruit produced a rubber knife and thrust the blade at her stomach. With the speed of a panther, Charley shifted off line and knuckle-punched the back of the boy's hand—her target a *kyusho* nerve point that sent a crippling stab of pain through the boy's hand, forcing him to drop the knife. Then Charley reached for his face, clawed her fingers into his eye sockets and wrenched his head back. At the same time, she side-kicked the back of his knee. The boy slammed into the wooden floor.

"Stay down!" hissed Charley. Terrified by her wildcat glare, the boy did exactly as he was told.

A moment later, Charley was charged by Sean, an ox of

a recruit. She stumbled backward under his assault. Overpowering her through sheer brute strength, he pinned her against the wall and clasped his hands around her throat. Charley spluttered for breath. But she didn't panic. Instead she swung an arm across and down onto his elbow joints. Sean collapsed forward under his own weight. Sliding aside at the last second, Charley drove him headfirst into the wall. Sean staggered away in a daze.

David now approached rapidly. Charley flicked her fingers in his eyes. Half blinded, David was unable to defend himself as she followed up with a kick to the groin. Although not delivered at full force, the kick was more than enough to drop her team member.

"That's for the smoke bomb," she whispered before moving down the line.

Having just witnessed David's excruciating takeout, José hesitated in his attack. Charley took full advantage of this: she slammed an open palm into his chin. The impact compressed his jaw and caused José to black out momentarily. He slumped to the floor like a rag doll—a perfect stun-then-run maneuver.

With six recruits down and three remaining, Charley felt both elated and exhausted. Her breath was ragged and her heart pumping hard. But her merciless onslaught of the others had knocked the remaining boys' confidence and she dispatched the next two with surprising ease.

Charley couldn't believe it. She was almost at the end of the Gauntlet.

Only Jason barred her path, and he didn't look at all daunted. He threw a lightning-fast punch to her head. Charley ducked beneath it, only to discover it had been a feint. With his other fist, Jason caught her in the stomach and all the breath was driven out of her. Doubling over in pain, Charley was helpless as Jason seized her neck. Once again she found herself in a lethal chokehold.

"Night-night, Charley," Jason taunted as he squeezed and blocked off her windpipe.

Charley knew there was little point in struggling—she couldn't match Jason's strength. With no oxygen in her lungs, she had less than ten seconds before she blacked out.

Fight smarter, not harder.

Following Jody's advice, Charley reached across and took hold of Jason's little finger. Hoping he'd forgive her one day, Charley wrenched it back until she heard a crack. Jason bawled in agony and instantly let her go.

"It's for your own good," she said, delivering his own line back at him before striding the last few feet of the Gauntlet unchallenged.

Behind her, the gym was littered with groaning and injured boys.

Charley couldn't help but smile at the sight. All her hard work and extra training had paid off.

"She broke my finger!" Jason cried in disbelief as he stared at his misshapen joint.

"Stop complaining, Jason," said Steve, inspecting the damaged hand. "It's only dislocated."

Without warning, he tugged on the little finger and re-aligned the bones. Jason let out a whimper and went white with pain and shock.

"Man up!" said Steve, giving Jason a pat on the shoulder. Then he headed down the gym to Charley. "Congratulations, that was a remarkable performance. Speed, aggression and technique—an unbeatable combination."

He extended a meaty hand to her. As Charley went to shake it, she noticed her instructor had kept his other hand behind his back.

Always expect the unexpected.

Letting her instincts take control, Charley swiftly ducked under her instructor's arm. At the same time, she kept a firm grip on his hand, rotating his whole arm until it locked out. Driving it upward, she forced him to flip over to prevent his elbow breaking. Steve landed with a heavy crash on his back. He stared up at her with a combination of pain and pride.

"You made . . . the grade," he wheezed as the bottle he'd been concealing rolled from his grip and across the floor.

From the doorway came the sound of slow but appreciative clapping.

"Charley, you've surpassed even my expectations," Colonel Black declared with a rare smile. "I believe you're ready for your first assignment."

21

Charley almost went into shock. It was only the second day of her assignment, but she couldn't believe what she'd just witnessed. It wasn't an attack, a kidnapping attempt or even a shooting. Her Principal, fifteen-year-old Salma bin Saud, had just decided to buy a leather Chanel wallet for more than a thousand dollars!

Charley knew that Harrods was one of the most desirable and expensive places to shop in the world, but she was truly stunned at the price tag—and even more taken aback by Salma's blasé attitude toward it. Then Salma spotted a matching handbag—a steal at just under two thousand dollars—and added this to her growing pile of luxury goods. This girl was spending money like water, not even batting an eyelid when the salesclerk rang up a final bill of several thousand dollars.

For the first time, Charley realized just how different this world was. Having been assigned as personal guardian to a

Saudi Arabian princess on vacation in London, Charley was getting a rare glimpse into how the super-rich lived. It was surreal.

As the salesclerk bagged the stack of purchases, Charley recovered from her initial shock and returned to her close-protection duties. While no specific threat had been identified for the princess, her status and sheer wealth made her an obvious target for criminals and kidnappers alike. Charley's eyes swept the department store for suspicious individuals and any possible danger. This being Harrods, there was ample security in place. Besides the discreet surveillance cameras and peak-capped security guards at the doors, Charley had spotted a number of plainclothes officers wandering the aisles, impersonating regular shoppers. Harrods was as safe a place as any in London. Still Charley remained in Code Yellow, the relaxed yet alert state she'd been taught to maintain as a bodyguard.

"Take those," Salma ordered.

Charley looked at the two neatly packed Harrods shopping bags, but made no move to pick them up. "I'm sorry, Salma, but that's not what I'm here for."

Salma glared at her. "You don't expect *me* to carry them, do you?"

Charley blanched. "I need to keep my hands free in case there's a problem," she explained.

"Then carry them in one hand," said Salma, her tone indignant.

Charley didn't know how far to push this. Her duty was to protect her Principal, not her Principal's shopping bags. Yet she didn't want to upset the princess and receive a bad report. As Charley considered her next response, Salma retrieved the Chanel purse from one of the bags.

"Fine, I'll carry this." She sighed, as if she was doing Charley a massive favor.

Charley had to bite her tongue. Her bodyguard training may have prepared her for physical assaults, terrorist bombs and bullet wounds, but it hadn't prepared her to deal with spoiled rich kids. Picking up the two bags, she followed Salma down the aisle and toward the escalator.

Charley whispered into her discreet lapel mic. "Bravo One to Delta One. We're coming out. North exit."

"Roger that," came the driver's reply in her earpiece.

As they approached the exit, a concierge gave a polite good-bye and opened the door. The two of them stepped out onto Brompton Road.

"Where's my limo?" demanded Salma.

Charley checked in with the driver. "He's stuck in heavy traffic," she explained.

"Well, how long will he be?"

"He's not sure. There's an accident blocking the road. I

suggest we go for a snack while we wait. There's an excellent Italian cafe nearby." Charley had already researched the Knightsbridge area in case Salma wanted lunch. And sitting in a cafe was less exposed than standing in the street.

"We have to *walk*?" asked Salma. She looked horrified.

"It's not far. Just around the corner."

Salma shrugged. "I suppose it will be an adventure."

Charley informed the driver of the new pickup point, then set off. Walking a step behind the princess, Charley kept a careful eye on all the pedestrians. Her nerves were tense. She had no intention of making a mistake on her first assignment.

They turned onto a quieter side street that led to the cafe.

"Excuse me! Is this yours?"

Salma stopped as a roughly shaven man in a sweatshirt and jeans approached. He held a silver ring. "I think you dropped it," he said with a smile.

Salma looked at it. "No, it's not mine."

"My mistake," said the man. His smile vanished as he produced a knife from under his sweatshirt. "That purse isn't yours either. Hand it over."

Salma stood frozen to the spot as the mugger snatched the purse from her grasp. "Payday," he growled, then waved the knife at Charley. "And the bags."

"Sure," she said, calmly holding them out to him. If she hadn't been carrying the princess's shopping, she could have reacted faster. But since she had the bags, she intended on using them to her advantage. As the mugger reached out, Charley let go and the bags dropped to the ground. The man's eyes followed them and Charley lunged forward. She struck him in the throat with the edge of her hand. At the same time, she seized his wrist, twisting his arm to force him to drop the knife. But, despite choking from the blow to his neck, the mugger managed to wrench free.

"You little rat!" he snarled.

In his pain and anger, he lashed out at Charley and she leaped away from the lethal blade. As he came in for a second attack, Charley pulled a small canister from her pocket. Bugsy had supplied her with several pieces of high-tech equipment, including a legal pepper spray. Depressing the nozzle, she sprayed red gel into the man's eyes. Blinded, he cried out and tried to wipe his face. This only spread the dye, making it worse. Charley side-kicked the man in the knee and he dropped to the pavement, bawling in agony. Without mercy, she stamped on his hand and kicked the knife away. Once sure he was no longer a threat, Charley gathered the purse and bags and guided the shocked Salma quickly away from the few amazed onlookers.

The limo pulled up at the curbside.

"Are you all right?" asked their driver.

"Fine," Charley lied, her heart pounding. Opening the passenger door, she ushered Salma into the backseat. Then, picking up the bags, she hurried around to the other side and jumped in. The limo drove off, leaving the mugger still writhing on the ground.

The two of them sat in silence.

Charley thought about calling the police. But she didn't want to cause any more distress or hassle for Salma, and by the time the police arrived, the mugger would be long gone. She scolded herself for letting the man even get near the princess. She should have been aware of him much earlier. The ring had been a ploy to distract them and put them off guard. It had almost worked too!

Charley noticed the princess's hands were trembling. "Are you okay?"

Salma nodded. "Is London always like this?" she asked, her voice almost a whisper.

Charley shook her head. "No, not as far as I'm aware. We were just unlucky."

"Shame," she said, turning to Charley with a timid smile. "That's the most exciting thing that's ever happened to me. I was hoping we could do it again."

Charley stared at the princess, dumbfounded.

Then the two of them burst out laughing, releasing the tension. Charley's heart was still thumping and her nerves buzzed with adrenaline. But she had to admit the act of protection felt almost as thrilling as catching a wave.

Only now, after taking out an attacker in real life, did Charley realize she was no longer a victim—no longer the vulnerable girl she'd been when her friend Kerry was abducted.

Now she was a force to be reckoned with.

22

"Was this hidden message your idea of a joke?" Kay demanded, her green eyes blazing at the producer, Don. "Because it *wasn't* funny!"

"Of course not," replied Don, visibly wilting under her ferocious glare.

The other record company personnel sat rigid and mute around the conference table in Dauntless Records' headquarters, watching the producer's mauling with a combination of fearful fascination and evident relief that it wasn't them.

"Then exactly how did it get on to Ash's song?" inquired Kay.

Don swallowed nervously. "I have no idea—"

"You're the producer, for heaven's sake! You were the one who oversaw the recording process!"

Running a hand through his greasy locks, he replied, "Play anything backward and you'll likely find something. People thought Led Zeppelin had inserted *Here's to my sweet Satan* into 'Stairway to Heaven,' but they hadn't. The message in Ash's song is just a coincidence—a phonetic reversal."

"That's hard to believe," said Kay.

"If you're suggesting the message was backmasked on to the track, then I certainly didn't do it."

"Could anyone else have tampered with the recording?" asked Harvey, the vice president of Dauntless Records, a sharp-suited man with a preened mustache and close-cropped hair.

Don shrugged. "It's possible but unlikely. They'd need access to the studio, and advanced knowledge of the recording process."

"The police suggested a zealous fan could have hacked into the system as a joke," said Joel, Ash's slick-haired and slack-dressed A&R manager.

"Well, the media believes it's a publicity stunt," said Zoe, the PR executive, immediately regretting she'd spoken at all as Kay turned on her. The firebrand of a manager was already furious with her for letting the story leak.

"Is it?" she demanded.

"No, of course not," Zoe replied. "But it has rocketed pre-orders for the album. Whoever did this has done us a massive favor."

"*Favor?* This is a serious death threat to my client."

"Kay, might you be overreacting just a little?" interjected

Harvey. "It seems an extravagant way to send that sort of threat."

"Well, explain the text message . . . and *this*." Kay laid a color photocopy of a letter on the table. Glued to the pink letter was Ash's face sparkling with stars and glitter, the words *no more encores!* scrawled in red across his features. "You think I'm overreacting, Harvey? This was written in blood. *Pig's blood*, according to the police report."

"Aww, that's creepy." Zoe grimaced.

Joel leaned forward to inspect the letter. "What sort of sicko slaughters a pig for ink?"

"Possibly the same one that sends hoax letter bombs and subliminal song messages," said Kay.

"Has Ash seen this?" asked Harvey, jutting his chin at the letter but not making any move to touch it.

Kay shook her head. "No. I'm having all his mail intercepted. He's got trouble enough focusing as it is."

"Do you think he's actually in danger then?" asked Zoe.

Kay nodded. "The threat against him is very real."

Joel coughed hesitantly. "You're not thinking of canceling Ash's US tour, are you?"

"Certainly not," replied Kay. "Pulling Ash out of the limelight at this point would kill his career. And I will not be dictated to by some maniac."

"Good," Harvey chimed in. "Besides, there's far too much money at stake to cancel."

"The tour security needs to be airtight," Kay declared, producing a document from a leather-bound folder and passing it to the vice president. "Here are Ash's protection requirements."

Harvey scanned the document. He looked shocked. "You don't expect us to foot the bill for this, do you? He's not royalty, you know."

Kay resolutely held his gaze. "Considering how much money Ash makes for your record company, he's royalty to you. And, as per the contract I negotiated, it's part of tour support."

Frowning, Harvey studied the document again, then pointed to a particular line. "What's this extra cost here for?"

"It's for a company that deals in specialized close protection," explained Kay. "They come highly recommended by my inside source on the military security circuit."

23

"Look who's back!" said Jason, ditching his dumbbells and toweling the perspiration from his face.

The rest of the team stopped their fitness training and turned to see Charley standing in the gym doorway. She was dressed in a running top and jogging pants, her hair pulled back in a ponytail, face drawn and eyes ringed with tiredness.

"How was Colombia?" asked Blake, leaving the treadmill to greet her with a sweaty hug.

"Tough." Charley sighed. She was exhausted after the long flight but glad to be back among the team again. It seemed as if she'd been away on missions forever. Each time she'd returned, Colonel Black had another lined up. Having completed five assignments in as many months, Charley was looking forward to a break—especially after the trouble she'd encountered in Colombia.

Jason eyeballed her. "Dislocate anyone else's fingers while you were away?" he growled.

Charley held his gaze. While the rest of the team's respect for her had grown with each successive assignment—as Jody had predicted, *Prove yourself and you'll earn their respect*—Jason still hadn't forgiven her for the Gauntlet incident. "No, but I did break a man's kneecap," she replied.

José laughed. "You're one kick-ass bodyguard!" he said, fist-bumping her.

Charley appreciated José's support, but it had been no laughing matter at the time. She and her Principal, Sofia, the daughter of the Colombian minister of justice, had been in her father's car when it was attacked by hit men from a notorious drug cartel. Charley had barely escaped with her own life. Sofia hadn't been so fortunate—as they'd fled, a stray bullet had hit her in the abdomen, and she was now in the hospital in critical condition.

Blake noticed the mournful look in Charley's eyes. "Are you all right?"

"Yeah," she lied. "I'm just a bit jet-lagged."

"I bet you're hungry after the long journey too," he said, putting a comforting arm around her shoulder. "Let's go for lunch. That'll make you feel better."

After freshening up, the whole team headed to the dining hall only to discover a line had formed.

"Who are all these people?" asked Charley, gaping at the unexpected line of kids.

"New recruits," David explained. "Guardian is expanding to meet demand."

"Yeah, fresh meat!" sniggered Jason.

One of the new recruits, a petite Asian girl with a bob of jet-black hair and a silver ring piercing through her left nostril, glared over her shoulder at him. "At least we don't smell like rotten meat," she said, wafting a hand in front of her nose.

Jason bristled at the insult. "Hey, pipsqueak, we just showered."

"With soap or manure?" retorted the girl, and everyone laughed.

Charley took an instant liking to her.

Jason clenched his fist. "Zip it, newbie, unless you want a fat lip."

The girl turned on him. "And how are you going to do that with your broken arm?"

Jason furrowed his brow in confusion. "I don't have a broken arm."

"Not yet." She squared up to him, even though she was half his height.

Jason puffed out his chest.

"Okay, let's chill," said Charley, stepping between them and smiling at the girl. "What's your name?"

"Ling," she replied, her dark eyes still blazing at Jason.

"Well, I'm Charley, and I can't tell you how glad I am not to be the only girl here anymore."

"Of course you're not," said Ling, pointing to a small group of girls at a table beneath the hall's main window. "You should join us, instead of hanging with this loser."

Charley was amazed at the sudden influx of female guardians at the school. Colonel Black had been true to his word after all. "Thanks, I'd love to. I just need to catch up with my team first."

"Sure," said Ling, flashing Charley a smile before narrowing her eyes once more at Jason. "Meathead here probably needs your help to eat."

Jason scoffed. "Can I borrow your bib and high chair then?"

Ling held up a clenched fist. "Eat this," she said.

As Ling strutted away to join the other girls, José and David exchanged astonished looks.

"She's a fiery one," remarked Blake.

Jason surprised them all by grinning and saying, "Yeah, I like her."

"Careful what you wish for," said José. "She might end up on your team."

"*Jason's* team?" exclaimed Charley as she chose her lunch. "What's happened to our team?"

"Given the number of new recruits, the colonel plans to split us into different squads—Alpha, Bravo, Charlie and Delta," explained José.

Charley frowned. "That's the first I've heard about it."

"He wants us experienced guardians to babysit the newbies," said David.

"Yeah, and by the looks of it they're gonna *need* babysitting," remarked Jason, nodding in the direction of a skinny Indian boy. "Where did the colonel find that beanpole?"

"Bodyguarding's not all about muscle," Charley told him.

"Well, let's hope his brains are bigger than his biceps, for his *and* his Principal's sake," muttered Jason, filling his plate with a mountain of pasta and sauce.

After lunch, Charley chatted with the girls before jet lag finally caught up with her. Yawning, she left the dining hall and headed up to her room. But she was stopped at her door by Blake.

"So, are you really okay?" he asked. "I heard from the colonel it was a pretty rough assignment."

Charley responded with a tired smile. "Yeah, it didn't exactly go according to plan."

"But you did your job and that's what counts," he said, trying to reassure her. When she didn't reply, he took both her hands in his. "I was really worried about you, Charley," he admitted.

"That's sweet of you, Blake. But I'm fine. It was my Principal who got shot." Charley felt a tightening in her throat. "I—I tried to give her body cover, but there were just too many bullets flying . . ."

Blake wrapped his arms around her and drew her to him. Charley closed her eyes and hugged him back.

After the smoke-bomb incident, their relationship had stalled for a while. But Blake had been persistent and, against her better judgment, the two of them had started dating. Charley had made it clear, though, that they needed to keep it low-key. She had no intention of being judged by their relationship rather than her ability as a bodyguard. Yet at moments like these she was deeply glad she had Blake. Assignments took their toll, and it was comforting to have someone she could talk to and rely on, even if they did barely see each other between missions.

Blake lifted her chin with his finger and stared into her eyes. "I missed you—"

"There you are, Charley!" called Jody. Their instructor bounded up the stairs, and the two guardians rapidly pulled apart. "The colonel wants to see you right now."

24

The colonel's office was a large wooden-paneled affair furnished with high-backed red leather chairs and a heavy mahogany desk. The faint aroma of polished wood and rich leather gave the room an aristocratic air. Yet the antique design and old-world atmosphere contrasted sharply with the state-of-the-art LED displays on the walls and the ultra-slim glass monitor on the desk's integrated computer system.

Charley stood at attention in the middle of the room. It took all her willpower not to just collapse onto the carpet. Her body was weary and stiff from the long flight; her thoughts were chaotic and strained from exhaustion, concern for Sofia and dread at what the colonel had to say about the mission.

Colonel Black wasted no time. "It's good news," he announced. "Your Principal Sofia's on course to make a full recovery."

Surprised and relieved by the news, Charley felt a huge

weight lift from her shoulders. "I thought she was as good as dead."

"Not at all—your quick thinking and first-aid skills actually saved her life," he explained. "Minister Valdez is deeply grateful for your bravery."

Charley forced a smile. "That's wonderful to hear, but I shouldn't have let his daughter get shot in the first place. I tried to give her full body cover, but there was simply too much crossfire—"

"Don't be so hard on yourself," scolded the colonel. "Without you, Sofia would most certainly have been kidnapped or killed."

He pointed to the monitor, where images of the crime scene in question scrolled past.

"I have the complete report here," Colonel Black explained. "The bullet ricocheted off the minister's armored car. You couldn't have done anything about it. We just have to be thankful it was a ricochet and not a direct hit. That slowed the bullet's velocity and stopped it from reaching her spinal cord. If you hadn't carried out emergency first aid at the scene, she'd have bled out. You acted like a true professional."

"It should have been *me* that took the bullet," she insisted, still feeling guilty.

"*Never* say that!" snapped the colonel. "A bodyguard with a death wish is a danger to everyone. Yes, we need to be willing to stand in the line of fire—but *only* if absolutely necessary to protect the life of a Principal. Charley, you need to value your own life as much as theirs. Remember, a dead bodyguard is no protection to anyone."

Colonel Black rose from his seat, stepped around his desk and laid a paternal hand on her shoulder. "I realize you're trying to compensate for not being able to save your friend, but you owe it to Kerry to forgive yourself."

Swallowing back the long-held grief for her friend, Charley blinked away a tear. "I know how crazy it sounds, but I felt that by saving others I could somehow bring Kerry back."

The colonel shook his head. "You don't need to save everyone, Charley. Nobody could do that. You've honored Kerry's memory a hundredfold with your commitment to bodyguard training and your heroic actions in the field."

The colonel pinned a silver shield with guardian wings to her T-shirt.

"What's this?" she asked, staring at the badge in puzzlement.

"For courage and outstanding performance in the line of duty," replied Colonel Black. "I consider you our top-ranking guardian, and you should be officially recognized for that."

Charley studied the shield, feeling a small flush of pride. This acknowledgment was proof that she was indeed the best of the best. She could almost picture her parents' proud smiles, if they'd still been around.

"Which brings me to your next assignment," announced the colonel, returning to his desk.

Charley blinked, her moment of glory swept aside by the prospect of yet another mission. "My next? But I just got back."

"Don't worry. You'll have ten days to prepare. But I thought you'd like to know who you'll be protecting . . ."

"Who?" Charley prompted when the colonel seemed to be purposely holding back on her.

"Ash Wild."

25

"The rock star?" questioned Blake the next day, his jaw dropping in astonishment.

Charley nodded with enthusiasm. "Yeah, I can't believe it either. He must be Guardian's most high-profile client yet."

"But he's a guy."

"Good observation skills," said Charley sarcastically. "Your point being?"

"Well . . . you've always been assigned to protect girls before," replied Blake.

"And? You've protected boys *and* girls on your missions."

"Yeah, but that's different."

Charley narrowed her eyes at him. "Why's it different?"

"Because . . ." Blake averted his gaze, clearly struggling to find a suitable answer.

"Because he's jealous, that's why." Jason smirked as he strode into the briefing room with the others and took his seat.

"No, I'm not," Blake shot back a little too quickly.

"Of course you are. Ash Wild is every girl's fantasy," Jason declared. "A super-rich famous rock star. You're no match for him."

"Nor are you, dingo breath!"

Jason held up his hands in defense. "Hey, I'm not competing for the same girl's affections."

His jaw tensing in anger, Blake started to rise from his chair.

Charley placed a hand on Blake's arm, urging him to sit. *So much for keeping our relationship low profile*, she thought. "For the record, I'm not interested in Ash Wild."

Jason gave her a look. "Yeah, right."

"I don't even like his music," she said. "Besides, that's a line we're not allowed to cross. Rule number one: never get involved with your Principal."

"Oops! I must have missed that one in the manual," Jason remarked with a roguish grin.

Charley stared at him. "Are you serious?"

Jason gave a noncommittal shrug. "It was only a kiss, and she made the first mo—"

"Oi, Casanova!" José interrupted. "Colonel Black's coming."

Everyone stood at attention as the colonel took his place at the head of the briefing room. He indicated for them to sit.

"Operation Starstruck," announced Colonel Black, wirelessly connecting his tablet to the overhead display and launching straight into the briefing. On the screen appeared a picture of a handsome teenage boy with brown hair and hazel eyes. "Our Principal is Ash Wild. British-born music prodigy, talented in guitar, piano, singing and songwriting."

"Well, that's a matter of opinion," mumbled Blake, slouching in his chair.

Ignoring his sullen remark, Charley powered up her tablet to take notes. She really couldn't deal with a jealous boyfriend, especially during a briefing. This was one of the reasons why she hadn't wanted to get involved with someone on her team. It just complicated matters.

"Not according to his chart success, Blake," Colonel Black countered. "Ash is the youngest artist ever to achieve a number-one album in the UK. He's topped the charts in sixteen other countries, including America, where he became the first British solo artist to enter the Billboard 200 at number one with a debut album. Now he's about to embark on one of the most anticipated US tours ever." Colonel Black paused and swept his gaze around the room. "Our job is to keep him alive on this tour."

"What's the primary threat?" asked David.

"An unidentified stalker, responsible for a hoax letter bomb and two death threats so far," the colonel explained as he presented the evidence on screen. "A nasty piece of hate mail written in pig's blood and a message hidden within Ash's latest single release."

"Yeah, I heard about that on the radio," said José. "Everyone thinks it's a PR stunt."

"Well, they're letting that story run, but it's not the case," replied the colonel. "I was contacted directly by Ash's manager, Kay Gibson." The display switched to a photograph of a striking red-headed woman in a black tailored dress. "Ms. Gibson, who happens to be Ash's aunt, is taking these threats *very* seriously. She's already upped Ash's normal security arrangements, adding more members to the team and making his personal bodyguard full-time."

The overhead screen filled with the image of a hulking three-hundred-pound man with a head like a wrinkled bowling ball and tattooed arms that could put a gorilla to shame.

José let out a whistle through his teeth. "He's one mean-looking BG! Any stalker's got to be crazy to take him on."

"What's his background?" asked Charley, suddenly feeling out of her depth in comparison to the colossal bodyguard.

"His name is Tony Burnett, known better as Big T," said the colonel. "He's old-school. Started out in security when he was a teenager, just like you lot. But he got his training at the school of hard knocks, working the pub doors in the East End of London, where he grew up. Later he moved on to concert security at the Hammersmith Apollo. From there, he toured with the likes of Iron Maiden, Black Sabbath, Slipknot and the Foo Fighters. Now approaching sixty, he's somewhat of a legend among music security professionals. That's how he acquired his position as Ash's personal bodyguard."

David raised a hand. "Why does Ash need Charley, or any other bodyguard for that matter, when he's already got Big T to protect him?"

"Big T will act as high-profile security, warding off the obvious threats," Colonel Black explained. "But Charley is needed for low-profile, discreet protection—to counter the unseen and unexpected dangers."

"But why choose Charley? Especially after her last mission," said Jason, glancing across at her. "Wouldn't it be better if I went? I could pretend to be one of the band."

He thinks he's One Direction, thought Charley, bristling at Jason's never-ending doubts about her ability.

"No," replied the colonel. "Charley has a distinct advantage over you. The fact that she's a girl will allow her to blend in better. Officially she will be on the tour as a PR intern, but to any casual observer she'll appear as just another Ash Wild fan."

"So does Big T know I'll be Ash's guardian?" asked Charley.

José laughed. "Yeah, better not step on the big man's toes!"

Colonel Black nodded. "Ms. Gibson informed him. As I understand it, he'll be the only other person in the entourage, aside from Ash and the tour manager, to know your true role."

Charley made a note of this as the colonel turned to the others on the team. "Blake, you'll be the prime point of contact for Charley here at headquarters."

Having sat silent throughout the briefing, Blake glanced up from his sulk and nodded.

"Jason, investigate Ash's background and run a threat assessment on him." A long series of dates flashed up on the screen. "José and David, this is the planned tour itinerary. Research each venue, hotel and location, so that Charley has instant access to maps and all other essential information."

"Yes, Colonel," replied José and David in unison, both opening up the tour file on their tablets.

The colonel turned back to Charley. "We have a meeting with Ash and his manager at the end of next week. Ensure you're fully prepped. Bugsy's updating your go-bag, so remember to stop by the logistics supply room. Other than that, you know the drill."

26

"Meet Amir," said Bugsy, introducing the skinny boy Jason had spotted in the dining hall the week before. "He's assisting me with mission logistics."

Amir stared wide-eyed at Charley from behind the work counter of the supply room, giving the impression he was a little in awe of her.

"Hi, I'm Charley," she said, leaning against the counter.

"I know," he replied with a timid but endearing smile. "Everyone knows who *you* are."

Charley raised an eyebrow. "They do?"

"You're quite a celebrity now, Charley," said Bugsy, dumping a light green backpack on top of the counter and unpacking its contents. He laid out the items in two rows, then stepped back.

"You explain what's in her go-bag, Amir," Bugsy encouraged, popping a stick of chewing gum into his mouth. "It'll be good experience for you."

Clearing his throat, Amir picked up the first item. "Well . . . this is a phone," he began.

"I can see that." Charley smiled.

"A smartphone, actually . . . It has all the usual features," he continued, his voice quivering slightly. "High-res camera, video capability, GPS, Internet . . . but it's also a weapon."

Now Charley was interested. "What sort of weapon?"

Amir pointed to two small metal studs at the top of the device. "A stun gun. Slide the volume button up a notch and simply press to deliver over three million volts of electricity . . ."

The ghost image of Kerry's tortured face and shuddering body flashed before Charley's eyes. She blinked and the vision was gone, but the chill of grief and guilt lingered. Amir was too involved in his description of the phone's workings to notice her brief pained expression.

"The shock will effectively short-circuit the attacker's nervous system, causing loss of balance and muscle control, confusion and disorientation. It's like being shocked by a cattle fence, only fifty thousand times stronger. Even through clothing, it can take out a fully grown adult."

He pressed the button; there was a fearsome crackle, and a blue bolt of electricity arced between the two studs. The boy grinned. "I like to call this device the iStun."

But Charley didn't laugh. Instead she quietly replied, "I know from experience what it can do."

"You do?" he said, stifling his own laugh when he saw her expression. "What happened?"

"I'd rather not talk about it, if that's all right."

"Sure, I understand," he replied with an earnest nod. "Client confidentiality and all that."

Amir put the stun phone aside and picked up a small aerosol can. "This looks like a standard deodorant. But in fact it's—"

"A legal pepper spray," Charley finished for him. "I used it on a previous assignment. Fires out a red gel that disorients an attacker and stains their skin."

Slightly crestfallen at missing an opportunity to explain this himself, Amir held up a tiny white box no bigger than a sugar cube instead. "Okay . . . how about the Intruder?"

"Go on," encouraged Charley. She felt bad after realizing Amir was trying desperately to impress their instructor. So she leaned forward and made a show of interest.

"This is a mini portable surveillance device," he explained eagerly. "Instant setup. Just fix it to a wall using the reusable adhesive on the back. If someone crosses the sensor's beam, the device instantly alerts your phone with a text message. Bugsy thought these would be ideal for detecting intruders while you're on tour."

Charley examined the box. "It's certainly compact."

Heartened by her approval, Amir moved on to the next set of items in the line. "Now, these are really cool! Bugsy got them custom-made."

"What's so special about a T-shirt?" asked Charley as he unfolded the first black garment and laid it out on the counter.

"It's woven from a high-tech super-fabric," he explained. "This T-shirt is not only fireproof, it's stab-proof too."

"Stab-proof!" exclaimed Charley, feeling the thick cotton-like fabric between her fingers and doubting its capabilities. "Are you sure?"

"Well, I haven't tested it *personally*," Amir admitted. "But Bugsy assures me it is."

Charley glanced at her instructor, who gave a single nod of his bald head. "Do you want to test it out?" he asked.

"No, it's fine. I believe you," Charley replied quickly as he began to unsheathe the knife on his utility belt. She returned the T-shirt to Amir.

"There's all your standard gear too," said Amir, sorting through her remaining equipment and repacking the items carefully into her go-bag. "First-aid kit, communications unit, flashlight—"

"What's this? A secret poison dart?" asked Charley, picking up a ballpoint pen from the counter.

"No," Amir replied, looking at her as if she had a screw loose. "It's just a pen. But I thought I'd include it in case your Principal is asked to sign autographs. You don't want to be hanging around, exposed any longer than necessary, while a fan searches for their own pen."

On hearing this, Charley reappraised the potential of the raw-boned boy. He might not have the muscles, but he certainly had the brains to be a bodyguard. "Good thinking, Amir."

Amir beamed at the praise.

"Actually, this *isn't* just any old pen," said Bugsy, stepping in and taking it from Charley. "The casing is made from high-impact hardened polycarbonate. This means it functions as a very effective self-defense weapon too."

Amir frowned. "How can a pen be used as a weapon?"

"Allow me to demonstrate." Holding the pen in an ice-pick grip, Bugsy said, "Like a Japanese *kubotan*, you can use this to strike at pressure points on the human body. The neck is the best place to target."

Without warning, he drove the tip of the pen into the clump of nerves just above Amir's collarbone. Amir let out an anguished cry and crumpled to the floor, where he lay gasping in pain.

"Highly effective, as you can see," said Bugsy, returning the pen to Charley.

Collecting her go-bag, she slowly shook her head at Bugsy. "No wonder no one ever wants to be your assistant!"

27

"New York, Dallas, Las Vegas, Miami, L.A.... Talk about one awesome assignment!" said Blake, loading Charley's travel case into the trunk of the Range Rover. "Wish I was going with you."

"You forget, all that traveling's a hard slog," replied Charley as she crunched across the gravel driveway with her go-bag.

"Yeah, right. Free concerts, celebrity-filled parties, exotic locations. I'd kill to go on a mission like that."

"Well, if you recall, I'm on this mission because someone wants to *kill* Ash."

"As if that's going to happen with all the security his manager's put in place."

"Don't underestimate the lengths celebrity stalkers will go to," said Jason, coming up behind them. "I've read some pretty disturbing stuff during my research into possible threats against Ash. Breaking-and-entering to lie in wait for the celebrity. Fantasies of torture and mutilation. Killing of family pets. Voodoo dolls sent in the mail—"

Charley rolled her eyes. "You're not going to scare me, Jason."

"You should be scared. Celebrity stalkers may seem like over-obsessed fans, but they're often deluded, mentally ill and can be violent—even deadly."

"Well, that's a cheery note to say good-bye on!" said Blake, closing the trunk.

"Have neither of you read my threat report?" asked Jason, indignant.

"Not yet," Charley admitted.

"Well, I wouldn't recommend reading it before bedtime. It'll give you nightmares." Jason offered Charley a half-hearted wave and strolled back inside.

"Man, he can be an idiot sometimes!" said Blake. Once certain Jason was gone, Blake reached tentatively for Charley's hand. "Listen, I'm sorry for being a little . . . grumpy with you lately. It's just that . . . I worry about you."

"I can handle myself," Charley replied, thinking, *Why did he wait until now to make his apology?*

"I know you can," he agreed. "And I admit it: I'm jealous. Ash is going to spend all that time with you and I'm not."

Charley squeezed his hand in response. "We always knew this would be difficult," she said. "We only get to see each other between missions. That's why we should try to make the most of it when I am here."

"You're right, of course." He moved closer, his expression hopeful. "Are we good now?"

Blake's sullen attitude since discovering she'd be protecting Ash Wild had been tiresome. It was hard enough preparing for a mission, let alone managing a moody boyfriend at the same time. But he *had* apologized . . . and he was cute. And it was reassuring to know she had someone back at the base who truly cared for her.

"We're good," she said.

Smiling, Blake wrapped his arms around her and drew her close. But, as he moved in to kiss her good-bye, there was a crunch of gravel behind them and they both turned to see Colonel Black making his way toward the Range Rover. They broke their embrace a second or two before he spotted them.

"Ready to go?" Colonel Black asked.

Charley nodded. The colonel clambered into the Range Rover and gunned the engine. As she jumped in beside him, she secretly blew Blake a good-bye kiss. "Save that for my return."

Blake caught it and mouthed in reply, *Stay safe.*

28

"The media has become so intrusive that celebrities have little privacy anymore," explained Kay, reclining in a designer chair, her long legs crossed beneath the oval glass table that she'd invited Colonel Black and Charley to sit around. "That's why we need exclusive residences like this."

She waved a hand at the stylish decor and plush furnishings. White leather sofas, black walls, the largest flat-screen TV Charley had ever laid eyes on and, most impressive of all, a teardrop swimming pool that started in the living room and finished outside in a landscaped garden enclosed by high walls topped with razor wire.

"Of course, it all costs money," Kay admitted, "but it's worth it to keep Ash safe."

"The security here is most reassuring," confirmed the colonel. They'd entered the West London estate through a manned gate, then had their IDs verified again by Big T at the door. Along with the razor wire on the walls, Charley had noted discreet surveillance and infrared cameras strategically located around the residence. There were even panic buttons installed in every room. The villa was a literal fortress.

"Has Ash received any more death threats?" the colonel asked.

"Nothing by mail since moving here," Kay replied. "So far we've managed to keep Ash's new address a secret and we're monitoring all the mail that does come in."

"That's good news," said Charley.

"It would be if that was the only source of threats." With an icy fury in her eyes, the music manager opened a superslim laptop and turned the screen toward them. "Like any celebrity, Ash is a target for online abuse. He receives a constant stream of insults and threats from haters eager to criticize, belittle, character-assassinate or worse. These sort of people make me sick!"

Colonel Black and Charley studied the sample of online posts on the screen. They varied from childish name-calling and scornful posts to harmful rumors and threats of physical violence. The messages became more and more extreme the farther down the page Charley read:

```
#AshWild's music is torture, someone
should torture him!
```

I'd punch his lights out if I could
#AshWild

You suck! @therealAshWild

"Of course, all this abuse is accessible to Ash," Kay said with a sigh. "I can't shield him from it."

"But *we* can shield him," stated Colonel Black. "It'll be a tricky task to sift the genuine threats from the trolls. But I'll have my team run a search of these users through the police database to establish if any of them have a criminal record or a history of violence. That should help identify potential suspects."

"Do you know anyone who might have a grudge against Ash?" asked Charley.

Kay tapped a polished nail on the glass table while she considered this. "There is one: a songwriter who's convinced Ash stole his hit song 'Only Raining' from him."

"Did he?" asked Colonel Black.

"*No*," Kay replied emphatically, then threw up her hands. "However, where there's a hit, there's a writ. The guy sued Ash and he was furious when he lost the court case, along with all his money paying the legal costs. His name is Brandon Mills. The police interviewed him over the letter bomb, but they found nothing that linked him to it."

Charley ran a quick search on the Internet and pulled up

an image on her tablet screen. "This him?" she asked, pointing to a middle-aged man with dark blond hair, designer stubble and steel-blue eyes. He looked like a wannabe George Michael.

Kay winced, then nodded.

"You know this man?" asked the colonel sharply.

The music manager's eyes narrowed. "We lived together. Briefly."

"And?"

"It didn't work out. Nothing to do with Ash."

Charley downloaded the image and associated links to the threat folder in her operation file, making a note of Kay's involvement with him.

"Anyone else?" asked the colonel. "One of Ash's ex-girlfriends, perhaps?"

Kay pursed her lips. "Ash has had a few girlfriends. Hanna Price was the latest, but she's busy with her own teen modeling career now. And she doesn't strike me as the vengeful ty–"

"Sorry I'm late," said Ash, strolling into the room. "Got stuck songwriting and lost track of the time."

He pulled out a chair and plonked himself down next to his manager. His smoldering eyes were enough to melt any girl's heart, and he used them to full effect on Charley along with a dazzling smile. But, having seen the exact same look in one of his publicity photos, Charley had no difficulty resisting his charm. She had to admit, however, that Ash had a certain star quality. When he'd entered the room, there was an instant frisson in the air, like a buildup of static electricity.

"So, you must be my new bodyguard," said Ash, addressing Colonel Black with a salute.

The colonel stared straight back at him. "No, Charley is," he said, pointing at her.

Ash did a double-take. "*Seriously?*" He laughed out loud, but when no one else joined in, it quickly petered out. "You *are* serious."

"Yes," said Charley.

"No offense," said Ash, "but you're, like, my age and a *girl*."

"That's the point," replied Charley, trying hard not to take offense. "The best bodyguard is the one nobody notices, and I can blend in as one of your friends or as a fan."

Ash responded with a strained smile. He leaned over to his manager. "When you said Charley, I thought you meant a guy," he hissed.

"Does that make a difference?" said Kay.

"Of course it does! How's *she* going to protect me?"

"*She* is a trained bodyguard," responded his manager.

Ash glanced doubtfully over at Charley. "But I already have Big T, plus a full security team. Why do I need her?"

Kay replied, "Your protection is my highest priority. I want all bases covered. And Charley will be your final *invisible* ring of defense."

"Invisible? It's nonexistent! If some maniac can get past Big T, they'll be able to take out a girl. I don't think you're taking my death threats seriously! This has to be a joke."

"I'm deadly serious," replied Kay.

"Then hire a *real* bodyguard."

"I have," said Kay, her tone hardening. "Do you question whether I'm up to the job as your manager just because I'm a woman?"

Ash shook his head. "Of course not."

"Then *don't* question her ability as a bodyguard."

Charley sat awkwardly with Colonel Black as this heated discussion took place in front of them. While Ash's initial reaction hadn't come as a complete surprise to Charley, it was a disappointment and not the best way to start an assignment. Still, she was heartened by Ash's manager's stated confidence in her.

"I can assure you, Ash," said the colonel, "that Charley is very much up to the job."

"Well, I'll believe it when I see it," replied Ash with a strained smile. He looked at Charley. "Sorry for any confusion on my part. But an easy mistake to make, eh? Big military guy. Cute blond girl. Who'd have thought *you* were the bodyguard? Anyway, I have a band rehearsal now, so

I've got to run. I expect I'll bump into you on the tour then?"

"I can guarantee it," replied Charley.

As Ash excused himself and headed out of the living room, Kay turned to Charley. "Ash is worth a fortune to a lot of people. He must be protected at all costs. Now that I've backed you up, you'd better not let me down, Charley."

"Don't worry," Charley replied, sounding as self-assured as possible despite the huge weight of expectation on her shoulders. "I'll accompany him like a second heartbeat."

29

Color posters swamped the four walls of the cramped little bedroom. Glossy calendars—some official, some not—were pinned alongside, while cutout magazine articles filled the remaining spaces. Not a single square centimeter of the original wallpaper was visible beneath the massive unbroken montage. Even the ceiling was blanketed in pictures, postcards and concert memorabilia.

Every photo, every image was of Ash Wild.

His face grinned out in perfect heartthrob style—performing at a concert, appearing on television, posing on the beach. Tabloid shots showed him going for a jog, having dinner, shopping for food, walking in the street, his whole life—professional and private—exposed by the lenses of a million cameras.

A full-size cutout of the rock star stood in one corner of the room. Creepily lifelike, the cardboard Ash watched over the most precious items of the collection: an Ash Wild baseball cap, a signed tour program, a limited-edition vinyl copy of Ash's first single, a guitar pick thrown by the star during a gig. And, at the heart of this treasure trove of souvenirs, a photo signed by none other than Ash Wild himself.

The bedroom was a virtual shrine to the rock star.

And, to leave no one in doubt, on the bedroom door hung a sign saying **I'M A WILDLING!**

The computer on the desk displayed a Wildling fansite— *Wild: For the fans by the fans*—updated seconds before with a new post gushing about the forthcoming tour. From the desktop speakers, on endless repeat, Ash's voice sang "It's only raining on you, only raining . . ."

The single bed, the only other piece of furniture in the room, was covered with an Ash Wild duvet and pillowcase. On top lay an open suitcase. Inside, clothes were folded neatly and packed in individual clear plastic travel pouches. A toiletry bag, containing shower gel, face cream, a hairbrush, deodorant, a blister pack of pills and a tube of toothpaste, was carefully stowed. And tucked inside a money belt was a slim stack of highly sought-after concert tickets, plus the necessary travel documents and a crisp new passport.

From downstairs came the sound of a doorbell ringing.

"Hey, sweetie, your car's here!" called up a shrill voice.

With a final check of the contents, the Wildling closed the suitcase, slipped on the money belt and rushed down to the waiting taxi.

30

"Sandy Higgs, ABC News," said the reporter, introducing herself. "Ash, your rise to fame has been meteoric. When was the first time you realized you were famous?"

"When I got my first death threat!" Ash replied.

A ripple of laughter filled the conference room in New York's Soho Grand Hotel. Ash sat relaxed in front of a microphone; behind him a huge backdrop of his face announced the start of his Indestructible tour.

"But, seriously, I'm not in this for the fame," Ash went on. "I'm in it for the music. And for my fans."

Charley stood just offstage, out of the limelight. She stifled a yawn, fighting the remnants of jet lag after the long flight from London Heathrow airport. It was the first official day of the assignment, and she was determined to be on the ball. She'd had little time to settle in or get her bearings, aside from checking into the hotel and catching a glimpse of the Statue of Liberty as her taxi had crossed the Brooklyn Bridge into Manhattan.

Beside her towered the monstrous frame of Big T. She'd been briefly introduced to the veteran bodyguard on her arrival, but received no more than a grunt of acknowledgment before the press conference had begun. She hadn't tried to strike up a conversation with him, since experience had taught her when to talk and when not to talk on an assignment.

"Harvey Lewis, *TeenMusic Mag*," called out another reporter. "Your face and album are everywhere. Your songs dominate the charts and airwaves. Are you worried about overexposure?"

"I think it's too late for that!" Ash joked, gesturing at the massive publicity image behind him.

Another round of laughter greeted his response. Charley saw that Ash was in his element. With all the attention focused on him, he shone like a true superstar.

"It's better to burn out than fade away, right?" continued Ash. "No, I'm not worried about overexposure. I love touring, traveling the world, seeing new places and meeting new people. That's the joy of being a musician. And I've just released an album of new songs that'll keep my fans happy, for a while at least."

"Sara Jones, Heaven Radio. You're known for your close

interaction with your fans. But surely that's an issue, given the recent threats made against you?"

"Not really. Anyone has to get past Big T first!" Ash gestured toward his colossal bodyguard at the edge of the stage. Big T put on a suitably hostile scowl, playing up his role for the cameras. The photographers seized the opportunity and snapped away.

A man in a blue shirt and jeans stood up from among the reporters. "Stephen Hicks, freelance. Ash, is it true you received a death threat written in pig's blood?"

A hushed silence descended on the room. This was clearly news to the other reporters as well as Ash.

Ash frowned. "No . . . not as far as I'm aware."

"Well, I have a reliable source that says you did." Sensing a story, the reporter pressed on. "How do you feel about your team hiding this letter from you?"

"W-what letter?" demanded Ash, his previous cool demeanor fracturing. He glanced sideways at Zoe for guidance. The Dauntless Records' PR exec shook her head in reply.

"Doesn't that make you question who you can trust?" asked the reporter.

Ash didn't respond, his eyes now darting nervously around the room.

"Don't you fear for your life on this tour? Are you going to cancel if you get another death threat?"

Ash gripped the microphone firmly in both hands. "Listen, there's always going to be haters, no matter what," he answered, a tremor entering his voice. "But *nothing* will to stop me from going on this upcoming tour!"

"Not even a maniac promising 'no more encores'?"

Realizing the reporter was out for blood and seeing Ash's troubled expression, Zoe stepped onto the stage and took over the mic.

"Thank you, everyone, for your time," she said, smiling brightly. "Press conference is now over. The tour commences this Friday at Madison Square Garden."

Ash left the stage. Donning a pair of sunglasses, Big T immediately took up a position next to the rock star and led him out of the room. Charley joined them, blending in as part of Ash's official entourage—a work-experience PR intern, if anyone asked.

They crossed the almost-deserted reception area in silence.

A flustered Zoe caught up. "Sorry about that," she said to Ash. "That reporter won't ever have access again."

"Why wasn't I told about the letter?" Ash demanded angrily.

"Kay didn't want you worrying."

"Sounds like I should be!"

"Don't be," said Big T, striding alongside. "You're safe as houses with me."

And me, thought Charley, keeping guard on Ash's other side.

"Thanks, Big T," said Ash, beginning to smile again.

Approaching the exit, one of the guys on Big T's security team took point and opened the hotel doors. Emerging onto the street, they were hit by a tidal wave of people—paparazzi with cameras blazing like strobe lights, teenage girls screaming like banshees, young boys fist-pumping the air and chanting, "ASH! ASH! ASH!" Tourists and bystanders flocked to the scene to witness the commotion. Overwhelmed by sheer numbers, the police were swamped by the ocean of fans who'd broken through the barriers.

Big T carved a path through the seething mass, a protective arm around his charge. Charley trailed behind. She shielded her eyes against multiple camera flashes and tried to scan the crowd for threats. But it was pandemonium. Never before had she tried to protect somebody in chaos like this. Disoriented, deafened and half-blinded, she could barely guard herself, let alone Ash, as the mass of fans swarmed around to get a piece of him.

A paparazzi guy with a buzz cut and two days' worth of stubble knocked Charley aside. She stumbled and almost fell to the pavement, where she would likely have been trampled in the crush. "Watch it!" she cried.

He turned on her. "You watch it!" he said in a nasal tone and flashgunned her with his camera.

Blinking away stars, Charley soon lost track of Ash. In fact, she lost track of everyone. Jostled all over the place, she could barely stay on her feet. The only recognizable landmark amid the storm was Big T. She spotted him, towering above the gaggle of girls, groupies and photographers. Immovable as an oak tree, he barely swayed as the crowd pitched and rolled around him. She fought her way over to him and relocated Ash.

The rock star, smiling and laughing, had paused to sign autographs and pose for photos.

"You all right?" asked Big T, barely glancing at her.

"Yeah," Charley replied breathlessly. "Had a run-in with a photographer."

"Careful," he warned. "Don't get on the wrong side of the pap. They'll make your life hell."

A girl squealed in delight as Ash signed her poster. Another began crying when he hugged her. Charley thought one fan was actually going to faint when he signed her arm with a heart.

"And what's your name?" Ash asked a boy with dark blond hair whose starry-eyed look suggested he might explode at being so close to his idol.

"P-P-Pete," he managed to reply, grinning broadly as Ash signed his autograph book.

Then Ash held up the boy's phone and took an impromptu selfie with him. Glancing at the result, he noted the similarity in their features and said, "Hey, you could be my twin brother!"

"Really?" said the awestruck boy.

"Well, apart from your blond hair and blue eyes, we could be identical."

The fan gaped at him, wide-eyed. "Perhaps we're related."

"In another life, my friend!" Ash laughed good-naturedly and patted him on the shoulder.

Then Big T was steering Ash toward the waiting limo. Charley fought hard to keep by their side, but a few feet from the vehicle, she was caught in a riptide of fans and dragged in the opposite direction. Digging an elbow into the girl in front, she forced the fan aside. But it was no use. Another simply filled her place. Meanwhile Ash was edging farther and farther away.

Then a meaty hand grabbed her wrist. Yanked through the pressing crowd, Charley was back beside Big T. "Keep up!" he grunted, his other arm shielding Ash.

Charley now stayed determinedly in his wake. As Ash disappeared inside the blacked-out limo, there was a surge of fans behind. At the same time, Big T let Charley through. Her foot caught on the door frame and she landed in a heap on the floor of the limo. The bodyguard slammed the door behind her, the driver automatically locking them in for safety.

As Big T waded around the vehicle to the front passenger seat, the fans pounded on the roof, the thunderous sound like an army of jackhammers. Humiliated by her unceremonious entry into the limo, Charley quickly pulled herself into the soft leather of the rear seat, straightened out her top and combed a hand through her disheveled hair.

Meanwhile Ash sat cool, calm and collected beside her. He gave her a smug look. "Welcome to my life!"

31

"You're not on the list," said the gruff security guard, barring entry through the artists' entrance to Madison Square Garden, the iconic circular arena topping Pennsylvania Station in the heart of Manhattan.

"But I'm a personal guest of Ash," Charley insisted.

The security guard, a large man with a beer belly, let out a snort of laughter. "So is every other Wildling."

He turned to the other two guards manning the entrance with him and rolled his eyes at Charley's pitiful attempt to gain entry.

"Listen—if you call his manager, she'll explain—"

"Don't push your luck, girly. No pass, no entry!" he snapped.

Charley sighed. This was all she needed. First day of the tour and she couldn't even access the venue. Having asked the security guard to check the guest list three times, she began to wonder if she'd been left off the list on purpose.

Following her failure in even the most basic close protection of Ash after the press conference the previous day, perhaps his manager had decided she wasn't up to the job and canceled Guardian's services. But, if that was the case, surely she'd have heard from Colonel Black by now?

Charley checked her phone. No messages. She tried calling Kay Gibson, but her phone went to voicemail. Charley approached the security gate again.

The guard squared up to her, his fists planted on his ample hips. "I told you to leave."

"Can you just radio Big T? He'll vouch for me."

"Oh, you're a friend of Big T's!" said the guard, suddenly all smiles. "Why didn't you say so?"

He shifted aside and waved her through the gate. But she hadn't taken two steps when the guard seized her by the wrist.

"Don't be so dumb!" he growled, pushing his pudgy face into hers. "As if Big T knows *you*."

"Ouch!" Charley exclaimed as his grip tightened.

"I've had enough of you and your stories, little lady," hissed the guard in her ear, wrenching her arm behind her back and marching her out. He was clearly enjoying his moment of dominance.

But Charley wasn't going to be strong-armed off the premises. What would Ash and Big T think when they heard about it?

Goaded by the man's bullying tactics, Charley threw her head back. The guard cried out as his nose crumpled under the impact. She then scraped the heel of her shoe down his shin before stamping on his foot. Spinning out of the arm-lock, she promptly twisted the man's arm and drove him to the ground. As blood poured from his nose onto the concrete, the other two guards rushed to his defense, one pulling out an extendable baton.

Charley released the man and stepped away, her hands held up in surrender. "Just call Big T."

"We'll be calling the police," said the other guard, closing in.

"No, you won't," grunted a voice. "She's with me."

The three men spun around to see Big T standing at the gate. They stood openmouthed as he waved Charley through the barrier.

"Here's your security pass," said Big T, handing her a plastic ID card on a lanyard. "Don't lose it."

Charley slipped it over her head. "Thanks . . . I wasn't on the guest list," she tried to explain.

"That's cos you're part of the crew, not a guest." He glanced at the guard with blood splattered down his shirt. "Well, you certainly know how to make an entrance."

"Sorry. He was a bit heavy-handed."

Big T strode off down the corridor with Charley following.

"They weren't going to let me in," she explained, wondering how much trouble she'd gotten herself into. "But at least it proves security is tight."

"Not really," said Big T. "Most of these venue guards are inexperienced jacket fillers who don't have a clue how to do their job properly. Back in my day, the security industry was for the elite. Now bullies like that idiot you decked pass two-week bodyguard courses and think they're Jason Bourne!"

Charley looked hesitantly up at the bodyguard. "Do you think I'm a 'jacket filler'?"

Big T stopped, eyed her intently, then laughed a deep throaty growl. "That press conference exit was some baptism of fire, eh? Listen, Charley, we've all gotta learn from experience. Anyone would be shaken when confronted by a mass of crazed Ash Wild fans for the first time. Mind you, if you can take down a two-hundred-fifty-pound guard like that, then I'd say you're up to the job."

He grinned at her, revealing a gold-capped tooth.

Charley smiled back, deeply relieved at his apparent approval.

"Here, these are for you." Big T handed her a pair of designer sunglasses. "Essential gear for celebrity protection. Stops you from getting blinded by paparazzi cameras. They're also good for hiding your line of sight," he added as she tried them on for size. "If an attacker can't see where you're looking, they don't know when to make their move. This gives you the edge over them."

They walked on, turned a corner and entered the main arena. Thousands of empty seats encircled a stage in the shape of a massive guitar. Suspended above like a futuristic battleship was a rig of spotlights, speakers and plasma screens. Swarming over the stage, a team of roadies and sound technicians were making their final checks for that evening's performance. The sheer scale of the operation took Charley's breath away.

"Twenty thousand screaming fans will be packed into this venue tonight," remarked Big T. "Any one of them could be a lunatic and it's our job to spot 'em and stop 'em."

32

"Check . . . one . . . two . . . three. *It's only raining on you, only raining,*" sang Ash into his microphone.

"That's good, Ash," responded the sound engineer over the monitors. "Now your guitar."

A tattooed roadie, his face swamped by a caveman-like beard, ran onstage with Ash's signature Fender.

"Thanks, Joel," acknowledged the sound engineer as the roadie checked that the leads were all plugged in.

Slinging the leather guitar strap over one shoulder, Ash let rip along the fretboard. A gut-shredding riff blasted out from two stacks of speakers towering over either side of the stage. The sound engineer tweaked the levels, then gave a thumbs-up.

"Okay, let's go through the 'Indestructible' routine one more time," announced the tour's choreographer.

A group of dancers joined Ash on stage. The drummer

thumped out the distinctive beat that started the song and the dancers launched into a tightly synced routine.

"*In-de-structible!*" belted out Ash as he simultaneously busted moves with the dancers.

"Isn't he amazing?" came a sigh.

Charley, who'd been watching the rehearsal from the stage's wings, turned to see a slightly plump girl gazing in awe at Ash. Though her brown eyes were over-mascaraed, her round face was pretty in a girl-next-door kind of way. Her auburn hair was brushed into a fine sheen, she wore a flattering summer dress and her hands were manicured with dark red false nails.

She smiled at Charley, revealing a set of braces that slightly spoiled the effect. "Hi, I'm Jessie! I don't think we've met."

Charley returned her smile. "Jessie? You run Ash's fan club here, don't you?"

The girl beamed. "Why, yes! How did you know?"

Charley didn't want to reveal that she recognized the girl's face from a file in the operations folder that listed all the key people associated with Ash Wild. Nor that she knew Jessie lived with her mother in Columbus, Ohio, and that she had a cat named Ash . . . Charley pointed to the lanyard hanging around the girl's neck instead. "Your guest pass told me."

Jessie glanced down at herself, then back at Charley. "Of course. So who are you?" she asked, squinting to read Charley's pass.

"I'm Charley."

With an admiring look at her athletic physique, blond hair and sky-blue eyes, Jessie said, "You're very beautiful. Are you Ash's ...?"

Charley shook her head. "No, I'm a PR intern."

Jessie smiled with what looked like relief, then her gaze returned to the performers onstage. "I've been following Ash since day one. I was like the first American to truly recognize his talent—set up his fan website here, spread the word, did everything I could to build up his following. And now look at him. His first US tour! I can't believe he's really here."

The song came to an end and the choreographer dismissed the dancers. Swigging from a bottle of water, Ash strolled over to where the two girls stood chatting.

"I see you've met my number-one fan," said Ash, wrapping an arm around Jessie's shoulders and giving her a hug. "This girl made me in America!"

Jessie blushed at the praise. "Not at all. It was your songs ... your voice ... your talent ..."

"Yeah, but without fans like you I'm nothing," admitted Ash. He turned to Charley. "That's why Jessie's joining us for the tour—the least I can do after all she's done for me."

Ash perched on a guitar amp. "So, Jessie, let's do that interview you wanted for the website."

Jessie looked startled. "What, now?"

"Why not?" he said. "It'll get more crazy later on."

Jessie fumbled for her smartphone and a list of questions from her bag. Ash smiled for the camera and Jessie began recording. Charley could tell the girl was nervous, as her hands were shaking while she held the camera.

"Let me do the recording," offered Charley.

"Thanks," said Jessie, passing over her smartphone. "So, Ash, you're finally here in the USA. How's it feel?"

"It's *wild*," he replied with a smile. "I never thought I'd be playing my first gig in the States at Madison Square Garden. It's a real kick."

Jessie glanced at her question sheet. "Have you managed to see much of New York yet?"

"Not really. It's full speed ahead when on tour, but I did get up the Empire State Building. Awesome view! I saw all the way to the Statue of Liberty."

"So, what are your first impressions of us Americans? Like, when you got off the plane and saw everyone there, what did you think?"

Ash ran a hand through his hair. "I was blown away. I couldn't believe there were so many people waiting for me. I only wish I could have gotten to meet them all."

"Would you say your American fans are any different from your fans back home?"

"Well . . . if the fans at the press conference were anything to go by, they sure know how to scream! My ears are still ringing."

Jessie checked her prompt sheet. "Now that you're so famous, if you want to see a movie with a friend, can you go out and do that?"

"It's a lot harder than it used to be," admitted Ash. "But I suppose I could, as long as I have my security with me." He shot a wink in Charley's direction.

"And who would you invite as your date?" asked Jessie.

Ash pursed his lips and tapped a finger to his chin. "Well, I'm single, so I'm open to suggestions!"

Jessie stared wide-eyed at him and for a moment Charley thought that she was about to volunteer herself. But the girl buried her nose back in her list of questions, asking a few more before ending with, "So . . . do you ever get stage fright?"

"Not at all," replied Ash, his eyes gleaming. "It's like I was born to perform."

33

Ash danced and sang his way along the fretboard of the guitar-shaped stage. As he shimmied farther and farther out over the arena's sell-out crowd, the screams of the fans intensified and Charley wondered if any of them could even hear Ash singing. Big T had given her earplugs as well as a comms unit for the concert, but she could barely make out the security chatter above the noise of the band and the fans' insane shrieking.

Reaching the end of the headstock, Ash pirouetted on the spot, then sprinted back down the oversized fretboard. As he hit the main stage, he slid on his knees, snatched up his guitar and launched into a searing solo. His high-octane performance whipped the crowd into an even greater frenzy.

Witnessing Ash live in concert for the first time, Charley began to understand the mania surrounding this rock star she'd been assigned to protect. Ash lived up to his boast: he was a born performer—a rare superstar with the elusive "X

Factor" that legends like Prince, Michael Jackson and Justin Timberlake had all possessed. No wonder Ash attracted so much attention . . . both the good and the bad kind.

Leaping back to his feet, Ash strode toward Charley's side of the stage. She stood in the wings with Jessie and the rest of the tour guests, all of them watching awestruck as Ash brought the song to its climax. His voice soared into the chorus: *"You light up my life. You light up my heart. You light up the moon and the stars and the dark . . ."*

As he sang this line, he locked eyes with her.

"He's singing to you!" cried Jessie excitedly.

Charley felt an inexplicable thrill race through her body. Then instantly quashed it, firmly reminding herself that she wasn't supposed to be watching Ash perform. Her duty was to keep an eye out for threats—not easy when captivated by his stunning showmanship.

Charley broke away from his gaze to refocus on the crowd. Scanning the front rows for potential "lunatics" as Big T had put it, she thought the screaming fans *all* looked a little crazy. Of course, she'd experienced her own crushes on pop idols and movie stars in her time. But, seeing it from the performer's perspective, only now did she appreciate just how hysterical teenage girls could get. Some were crying with joy, their mascara running in black streaks down their faces. Others were frozen in openmouthed shrieks, like multiple copies of Edvard Munch's painting *The Scream*.

Many were jumping up and down as if electrified, while the remainder simply stared in simpering devotion.

With a crowd so demented, Charley was glad for the security guards posted at regular intervals around the arena. Given half a chance, the overenthusiastic fans would likely mob the stage and smother their idol to death.

Beyond the first few rows, the crowd turned into a sea of diminishing faces in the dark. There was no hope of Charley spotting a threat out there. That was the responsibility of the other members of the security team.

Before the concert, Big T had taken Charley on a tour of the arena as part of his security sweep. "Large venues with lots of people should always come with a health warning," he had explained as they'd walked the corridors and service tunnels of the building. "Any hint of a fire or an emergency and big crowds can turn dangerous very quickly. That's why you should always familiarize yourself with a venue. Know where your exits are. The best evacuation routes. And the designated locations for transporting the VIP. Some venues are like rabbit warrens and, trust me, you don't want to get lost in a crisis."

Charley had followed his lead, observing as the veteran bodyguard spot-checked emergency exits, identified potential security weak points and allocated postings for his team of guards. So she knew that the crowd was covered throughout the rest of the venue as best it could be. Backstage was even more secure, since an official photo pass was required to gain access. Big T had made it Charley's responsibility, along with another bodyguard stationed in the opposite wing, to stop anyone who mounted the stage from reaching Ash.

The fans cheered, whooped and clapped as the song "You Light Up My Life" came to an end. The backing band immediately struck up the next number—"Indestructible"—and Ash leaped into the choreographed routine with several dancers. The beat was infectious, and Charley couldn't help glancing at Ash's impressive moves. That's when she noticed a red bead of light in the middle of his chest.

A moment later it was gone. Had she imagined it?

Ash danced across the stage, whirling around with one of the girls. Then, as he stopped on the beat, the red dot appeared again. Charley didn't remember seeing the light during the rehearsal earlier that afternoon, and she was certain it wasn't part of the show. To her, the small red dot looked like the laser sight of a rifle.

Caught in the haze hanging over the stage, Charley followed the beam's path up into the darkness. The laser didn't originate from the lighting rig. It came from one of the private corporate boxes, a box she knew from their security sweep was closed for refurbishment.

Charley stepped away from the other guests and thumbed her comms unit. "Charley to Big T, code red. I think someone has a gun."

There was a crackle in her earpiece. "Big . . . *crzzzr* . . . say aga . . . *crzzzr*."

Charley repeated her warning, but interference was breaking up the signal. She tried shouting to one of the security guards near the stage, but the noise of the concert drowned out her voice. And the bodyguard in the opposite wing was too distracted by one of the pretty dancers to notice her madly waving for his attention.

As Ash danced, the laser beam tracked him across the stage. It leaped and spun, working hard to stay on target. The music stopped and Ash froze in a dramatic pose, one fist raised to the sky.

"*In-de-structible!*" he cried.

The red dot came to rest in the middle of his chest once more. Ash was oblivious to the threat as he basked in his fans' applause.

No more encores, thought Charley, recalling the ominous death threat.

With perhaps milliseconds before the shooter pulled the trigger, she dashed onto the stage.

34

Charley was first blasted by the noise of the crowd, then hit by the heat of the spotlights as she raced past the dancers. The stage suddenly seemed to stretch before her, and she prayed she'd reach Ash in time. The red laser dot remained fixed on its superstar target.

"What the hell?" cried Ash as Charley leaped on him, breaking the beam.

Shielding Ash with her body, she bundled him offstage to the shocked screams of his fans. Ash was too stunned to resist at first, but quickly regained his senses.

"Let me go!" he shouted, struggling in her grip.

Only when she reached the safety of the opposite wing did she release him.

Ash glared at her. "Have you gone completely insane?"

"You were about to get *shot!*" replied Charley.

This news shocked Ash into silence. He reached out to a nearby speaker for support.

"What in God's name is going on?" demanded a squat black guy with a trimmed mustache and shaved head. Terry was the tour manager, a hard-nosed, flinty-eyed man with a reputation for running a tight ship on tour. He hated any disruption to the schedule.

"A red laser sight was targeted on Ash. Someone was about to shoot him," explained Charley.

Terry frowned. "Did anyone else see this laser?"

The group of road crew, dancers and musicians who'd gathered around Ash and Charley all shook their heads.

"Did you see it?" Terry demanded of the other bodyguard as Big T came hurrying along the gangway to join them. He was a little out of breath, and perspiration shone on his bald dome.

The bodyguard, a blond-haired hunk with a chiseled jaw, crossed his bulging arms and grunted a definitive "No."

Realizing her credibility with Big T was at stake, Charley said, "Of course you didn't. You were too busy eyeing up that dancer."

The bodyguard shot her a dirty look. "Who is this girl?" he sneered.

"A PR intern," cut in Big T. "Now, let's establish if Ash is in danger or not. Charley, did you actually see someone with a gun?"

Charley shook her head. "I spotted the laser sight, that's all."

There was a groan of irritation from the band and road crew.

"Did *no one* else see it?" she asked, her tone almost pleading. "It was following Ash around the stage!" She was met by blank and hostile looks.

"It was probably one of the stage lights," said the bassist.

"Yes, most probably a stage light," agreed the tour manager, his eye twitching as he barely kept his anger in check.

"No. It wasn't," said Charley. "The beam came from a corporate box. The one closed for renovation."

Big T radioed up to one of his team to check out the box. The group stood in tense silence as they waited for a response. In the main arena, the bewildered crowd started chanting Ash's name, at first with enthusiasm, then with growing impatience.

"The box is empty. No one there," came the reply eventually.

Everyone stared accusingly at Charley. As a flush of humiliation reddened her cheeks, she wished the ground would just swallow her up.

"False alarm," Big T confirmed.

"On with the show!" ordered the tour manager, shooing people away with his hands.

Ash shook his head angrily at Charley, then strode back on to the stage.

"Hey, you fans are crazy!" he called out to the whistles

and cheers that greeted his return. "Next time one of you wants a hug, just ask!"

This offer sent the crowd into a near meltdown and almost lifted the roof with shrieks of delight. With a nod to the band, Ash kicked off the next song and the set resumed.

The stage wing quickly emptied as the crew returned to their duties. Charley remained where she was, her head hung in shame. She'd screwed up again! How could her judgment be so off? She was acting like a rookie on her first assignment. But she *knew* what she'd seen: a laser sight tracking Ash's every move. Her gut instinct had told her to act—if she hadn't, Ash might now be lying on stage in a pool of his own blood!

On the other hand, perhaps it had just been a harmless trick of the light, a reflected beam from the show or some other stage effect. Either way, the threat had come to nothing.

"We all make mistakes," said Big T, his tone surprisingly sympathetic.

"Not this big," she replied, unable to meet his eye.

As the dancers congregated in the wing for another routine, Big T took Charley to one side.

"I don't doubt you saw a laser, but it's most likely to have been one of these," he said, pulling a small silver pen-sized pointer from his pocket. He pressed a button and a red dot appeared on the floor. "These things are banned from concerts, but people still smuggle them in."

"I'm a complete idiot!" said Charley, holding her head in her hands. "How could I have thought that was a laser gun-sight?"

"Don't be so hard on yourself. To the untrained eye, there's virtually no difference between the two," he said, pocketing the laser pen.

Charley wondered why the old bodyguard was being so understanding about her monumental mistake. She'd disrupted Ash's first night of the tour, potentially blown her cover as his secret bodyguard and made enemies of virtually everyone on the crew.

"Did you know I was once Stevie Wonder's personal bodyguard?" revealed Big T. "Didn't last long, though. On my second night, I was guiding him up to a podium, didn't spot a loose cable and he tripped. Fell flat on his face. Even in my early days as a bouncer I never managed to put someone down so quickly."

Charley looked up into his heavily worn features. "That must have been awkward."

"Yeah, it was a real bummer," Big T admitted. "After that, I was guarding the toilets for the rest of the tour!"

Charley let out a heavy sigh. "I suppose that's what I'll be doing then?"

"No, Jon will be," he said with a fierce glare in the direction of the blond-haired bodyguard. "He should have been keeping his eye on Ash, not that redhead."

"So you're not throwing me off my assignment?" asked Charley, astonished.

By way of an answer, Big T showed her the tattoo on his inner forearm: *Only the paranoid survive.*

"As a bodyguard, this is a useful code to live by. I'd rather you overreact than not react at all," he explained. "When I started out, there was no training. Just thinking on your feet and learning from your mistakes. And, believe me, I made a truckload. But each mistake taught me something. You see, good judgment only comes from experience—and much of that experience comes from bad judgment. Live and learn, Charley, live and learn!"

35

"It's all across the Internet," said Blake, speaking to Charley on her smartphone the next day.

Charley groaned. The nightmare wasn't over for her yet. Backstage the road crew were preparing for Ash's second night at the arena, everyone giving her odd looks and a wide berth as they went about their business.

"Don't worry," Blake continued. "The only footage of the incident shows a flash of blond hair, then you and Ash were gone. It was a textbook-perfect extraction of a Principal."

"So my cover's not blown?" she asked.

"Not by the looks of it. All any photographer got was the back of your head. The story is that a Wildling jumped Ash in a fit of starstruck excitement. What spooked you anyway?"

"A laser dot. Thought it was a gunsight," she admitted. "But I was wrong. In fact, everything seems to be going wrong on this assignment. First the press conference, then the security guard and now this—"

"Whoa, hang on! What guard?" interrupted Blake.

Sighing, Charley explained the incident that had occurred when she'd tried to gain access to the venue.

"You head-butted a security guard!" laughed Blake. "You're out of control!"

"Thanks," she replied flatly. "That's what everyone here thinks too. And after last night I've ruined any chance of gaining Ash's confidence. He now thinks I'm paranoid. A liability. He hasn't let me anywhere near him all day. How am I supposed to protect him? The only person showing any faith in me is Big T."

"Best person to have on your side."

"I suppose so," said Charley, pacing the corridor outside Ash's dressing room. "I've been learning a lot from him about celebrity protection. He really knows his stuff."

"He should," said Blake. "He's been in the game long enough. And that's what you have to remember. This may be your sixth assignment—more than any other Guardian recruit—but that's nothing compared to his experience. Hang in there, Charley. I'm sure as the tour goes on, things will calm down. Just keep your head in the game and do the best you can. I have faith in you too."

"Thanks, Blake," she replied, feeling better with his support. "I miss you, by the way."

"Yeah, I mi—"

"Charley!" called out a gruff voice.

Covering her phone with a hand, she turned to see Big T's bulky frame heading down the corridor toward her. "You need to hear this," he said.

Blake's muffled voice sounded from the phone's speaker. "Charley, are you still there?"

She took her hand away and put the speaker to her ear. "I'll call you back."

Ending the call, she slipped the phone into her pocket. Her mouth had gone dry and her chest tightened at Big T's approach. She feared that he'd reassessed her actions in the cold light of day—and the conclusion wasn't good.

"What's up?" she asked.

Big T scratched at the stubble on his chin. "I just heard from the venue manager that the corporate box being renovated was broken into last night. Also, the fire exit nearby had been jammed open."

Charley's jaw went slack. "You mean . . . I was right, after all?"

Big T gave a noncommittal shrug. "We have no proof of a shooter, but there was certainly an intruder. I'm taking no chances tonight. There'll be guards patrolling the boxes. Terry's been updated and it's gone a long way to easing his concerns about you. I've informed Ms. Gibson too."

"Thanks. What about Ash?"

"I'll tell him after tonight's show. Best let him focus on his performance rather than worry about getting shot or not."

As Big T strode off, he patted her on the back with one of his meaty hands. "Good work, Charley."

Charley allowed herself a smile. Her gut reaction hadn't failed her. There *had* been a threat to Ash's life. While it wasn't good news for Ash, it did mean her actions onstage were justified. The tension she'd felt in her chest subsided.

Pulling her phone from her pocket, she was about to dial Blake's number when the door to Ash's dressing room burst open and his bassist rushed out. His eyes were wide with panic.

"Charley, come quick!" he cried, seizing her by the arm.

They ran into the dressing room. The other members of the band were crowded around Ash, who lay on the floor not moving.

"What happened?" Charley demanded, hurrying to his side.

"I don't know," replied the bassist. "He simply collapsed."

The drummer knelt beside Ash's prone body. "He's not breathing!"

"Move back, everyone," instructed Charley, trying to get a grip on the situation. *Dr. ABC* flashed through her head. There was no apparent danger. The floor was clear and Ash wasn't touching anything electrical.

She knelt down next to his head. "Ash? Are you all right?"

No response.

She gently shook his shoulder. Still no response.

Airway was next. After checking that nothing was block-ing his mouth, she tilted his head back and lifted his chin to open his airway. Then she placed her cheek close to his mouth and nose and looked up and down his body for any signs of breathing. She waited ten seconds but felt and saw nothing. A spike of alarm shot through her.

"Call 911," she ordered. "We need an ambulance *fast*."

While the bassist fumbled for his phone, Charley as-sessed Ash's circulation. There was no obvious sign of bleed-ing. She checked his pulse. A little fast but strong. That was a good sign. But he still wasn't breathing.

Pinching Ash's nose, Charley took a deep breath and bent over him. But before she could begin CPR, Ash opened his eyes and tried to kiss her.

Charley leaped away in shock.

"Sorry, I couldn't hold my breath any longer!" gasped Ash, sitting up.

"Now that's what I call mouth-to-mouth resuscitation!" cracked the bassist, having taken a video of the hoax with his phone.

The other band members were all apparently in on the joke. They laughed heartily.

"I thought you were dying," Charley exclaimed, glaring at him.

Ash grinned mischievously. "One false alarm deserves another!"

Charley was too stunned to reply.

"Oh, don't be such a sourpuss," he said, getting to his feet. "Most girls would give their right arm to kiss me."

Now over the initial shock, Charley felt a surge of anger at being duped. She was even more outraged at Ash's arrogance that he imagined she'd want to kiss him!

Charley responded with a tight smile. "How lucky I am." Then she drew closer and whispered in his ear, "You *ever* try to kiss me again, I'll break your arm."

Ash laughed it off. "Worth the risk!"

He waltzed out of the door with the rest of his band, their laughter echoing down the corridor as they headed for the stage.

36

Big T checked his watch and yawned. "The older I get, the more I hate these after-show parties," he grumbled.

Charley stood beside him as he guarded the entrance to the four-story town house that had been reserved for the sole use of Ash and his entourage. Even Charley was fading at three in the morning. She'd been invited to join the party, but after Ash's ridiculing of her she was keeping a professional distance—far enough away to be unnoticed, but close enough to react if there was any trouble. Meanwhile, Ash and his band were still grooving on the dance floor with a group of VIP guests: local celebrities, TV personalities and lucky fans picked out from the audience by the security team. The band was so pumped up on adrenaline from the concert that they needed to let off steam before heading back to the hotel to sleep.

"I heard about Ash's prank," remarked Big T over the heavy drum and bass of the DJ's music.

Charley grimaced with embarrassment. "Yeah, I'm sure everyone did," she said bitterly.

"Don't take it personally," he said. "Tour pranks are something of a tradition. When I was working security for Black Sabbath, Ozzy once poured Tabasco sauce into my mouth while I was sleeping! I sure woke up fast. I thought my tongue had been set on fire! I vomited all over the bed."

"Well, Ash was lucky I didn't vomit over him," replied Charley, glaring at the rock star, who was encircled by a gaggle of swooning young fans.

"Don't worry—I'm sure you'll get your chance for payback later in the tour. I certainly did with Black Sabbath."

"You did? How?"

Big T grinned. "I replaced the contents of a stick-on air freshener with raw chicken and hung it in their tour bus. After a few days, the rotting meat began to smell. Really bad. But nobody on the bus could figure out where the stink was coming from. The air freshener was the perfect disguise. The band spent the rest of the tour reeking of rotten chicken!" He let out a belly laugh at the memory.

Hearing this tale from the old bodyguard, she realized Ash's prank was just part of touring life and began to feel better. However humiliated she'd been at the time, she had to take it on the chin. Besides, from her training, she knew she had to give as good as she got—and she vowed she would when the opportunity arose.

Situated three floors up from the entrance, Charley looked down through a window at the street below. A crowd was still gathered outside. The location of the after-party had somehow been leaked. "Don't they have homes to go to?" she remarked.

Big T eyed the crowd. "Paparazzi never sleep."

Charley spotted a face she recognized. Unshaven with a hook nose, close-set mud-brown eyes and a buzz cut of black hair, it was the photographer who'd flashgunned her outside the press conference.

"Do you know who that guy is?" asked Charley, pointing to the man through the glass.

Big T snorted his disgust. "Yeah, that's Gonzo."

"Gonzo?" queried Charley.

"His real name's Sancho Gomez, but he looks more like the Muppet Gonzo to me. He's one of the paps that follow Ash around the world. In fact, he's the worst of them—a piece of scum, a former gang member turned freelance photographer. Guys like him should be called the stalkerazzi!"

"Can't you get rid of him?"

Big T shook his head. "Nothing we can do. Those guys justify their presence by citing the rights of freedom of the press. But ultimately it's all about the money."

"What money?" asked Charley.

"Paparazzi can earn tens of thousands of dollars for a single photo, sometimes even more. That's why they're so determined and desperate, Gonzo in particular. I hear he owes a large gambling debt to the mob. But, lucky for him, some tabloids are willing to pay six-figure sums for a unique shot."

"What do you mean by unique?"

"Anything that's a scoop, like a new relationship," explained Big T. "Or a picture that makes the celebrity look bad. And, if they can't get their shot naturally, they'll try to goad the celebrity into losing their cool."

Charley reappraised the group of paparazzi hanging outside the club. They were beginning to look more like a pack of sharks awaiting their prey. "So what can we do to stop them from getting that shot?"

"Not much. Just have the patience of angels," Big T replied. "No matter how rude they are, how much they push and shove or shout and scream at you, always keep your cool and a smile on your face. Remember, the key rule is to keep moving. Never stop among a pack of paps. Otherwise they'll eat you alive. If you do need to block a photo for any reason, simply put your body in the way. *Never* put your hand up to the lens."

Charley frowned. "Why not?"

"It'll give them a dramatic picture of your hand looking very large and very menacing in the lens. And then they'll have the story they were seeking: *Violent bodyguard attacks innocent photographer.*"

Ash strutted up to them with two starstruck fans. "Having

fun?" he asked. He swayed to the beat of the music, clearly still buzzing from the concert.

Ignoring the two giggling girls, Charley responded with a thin tight smile. "*You* seem to be."

"Here, check this out!" Ash proudly showed her his left forearm, upon which glistened a fire-red tattoo of a phoenix.

"Nice," said Charley in a noncommittal tone.

Ash leaned close to her ear. "It's only temporary. Be gone by the end of the tour."

"Come on, Ash," pleaded one of the girls, taking his hand as she shot Charley a jealous glare. "Let's dance some more."

Big T glanced at his watch. "Sorry, but we have to get the rock star back to his hotel by three thirty. It's ten past," he told them in a polite yet firm tone.

Ash shrugged. "Guess the party's over, girls," he sighed, flashing them a winning smile. They giggled and swooned as they tottered away. Charley rolled her eyes.

The rest of Ash's band and entourage joined them at the door.

Big T raised an eyebrow at Charley. "Time to meet the great unwashed!"

The cool night air hit them as they emerged onto the street. Immediately the paparazzi pounced. They swarmed around Ash, some even fighting one another to get in position for the best shot. Flashes burst like fireworks in the night. But Charley was more prepared for the craziness this time. Even though it was dark, she wore her sunglasses against the blinding flare of multiple cameras on full auto. And she kept her footing despite the mayhem of pushing and shoving.

"Make way, please," called out Big T, cutting a path through the throng.

"Ash, over here!" shouted a photographer.

"Look this way, Ash!" cried another.

But Ash kept his head down and followed in Big T's wake.

"Excuse me," insisted Big T, positioning his ample frame to shield Ash from the onslaught of photographers. However, the paparazzi proved experts at walking backward while taking their shots.

"Up past your bedtime, Ash?" teased a pap.

"Who were the two girls in the window?" asked another.

"None of your business!" he snapped, obviously annoyed at the line of questioning.

With the paparazzi becoming more antagonistic, Charley moved closer to Ash, protecting him from behind while appearing like a hanger-on of his entourage.

"Got a thing for blondes now, have you?" taunted Gonzo, his ratty eyes fixing on Charley. There was a brief flicker of recognition. "*Hola*, blondie. Are you his latest girlfriend?"

"No, just PR," she replied with a smile.

"Yeah, *suuure*. I believe you, chica. How about a picture of you two lovebirds together?"

Charley kept moving. Gonzo shoved a camera in her face and reeled off several shots. He was invading her body space, but she held her smile and didn't slow her pace.

More taunts and insults were hurled at Ash in a bid to spark a reaction, but Big T swiftly escorted the rock star into the awaiting minivan. Charley clambered in with the rest of the entourage, and Big T slammed the door shut. The paparazzi flocked around the vehicle, pressing their lenses against the tinted windows and assaulting the van with camera flashes.

As Charley took her seat, she heard Big T's voice in her earpiece.

"See what I mean? Those guys will do anything to get their shot."

37

It hadn't taken long. All the instructions were there on the Internet—even a helpful video.

The ingredients had been bought easily and without suspicion. Sugar and a frying pan from the supermarket. Saltpeter from the fertilizer section of a garden center. A small flashlight bulb, a nine-volt battery, a relay switch and some electrical wire from a hardware store. Finally, a large can of Hurtle high-energy drink and a cheap digital watch from a gas station.

The sugar and saltpeter had been mixed in a bowl at the exact ratio specified on the Web. Then the white powder was tipped into the frying pan and "cooked" over a low heat. As the mixture was constantly stirred with a wooden spoon, the grains of sugar had started to melt and caramelize. Gradually the white powder liquefied into a light brown paste with the consistency of peanut butter.

The resulting gooey liquid had been poured into the

now-empty energy drink can. As this mixture was left to cool and harden, the back of the digital watch had been pried open, its alarm buzzer disconnected and electrical wires attached. A circuit had then been made with the battery, relay switch and bulb.

With great care, the glass of the flashlight bulb had been broken to expose the filament. The delicate wire was buried in a small paper wrapper of uncooked sugar and saltpeter and inserted into the opening of the soda can. The watch and battery were taped to the outside of the can.

All the key components were now in place: a timer, a battery, an igniter and an incendiary mix—small enough to conceal in a backpack.

The bomb was complete.

38

Charley reclined in the upper-front lounge of the double-decker bus as it headed west toward Pittsburgh and Ash's next stop on the tour. She'd never been in a vehicle like it before. The tour bus was like Doctor Who's Tardis. There were sixteen curtained-off bunk beds, three separate lounges, a fully equipped kitchen and a designer-styled bathroom complete with its own shower unit. The lounges were upholstered in sumptuous black leather and boasted high-definition TVs, video game consoles and top-of-the-line sound systems. Charley would have believed she was in a high-class hotel if it hadn't been for the subtle sensation of movement and the suppressed noise of traffic outside.

Ash was downstairs in one of the air-conditioned bunk beds, catching up on sleep. When she'd passed him earlier, Charley had contemplated pouring Tabasco sauce into his mouth. But fortunately for him there wasn't any in the kitchen. Leaving the superstar to get his beauty sleep, she'd made her way upstairs, where she found the drummer and bassist absorbed in a two-player shooter game. A can of soda in hand, she'd settled herself in the sofa by the front window.

Gazing out at the traffic, service stations and fast-food joints that whizzed by, Charley's thoughts turned to the tour that lay ahead. There were still some twenty dates and a whole continent to cross. This bus would be their home for much of it and the one place that Charley could relax from her duties protecting Ash. That's if he *let* her protect him. At the moment he still seemed to consider her some sort of joke. But the threat against him wasn't a joke. His stalker could strike at any point on the tour. And she'd have to be ready, whether Ash took her seriously or not.

"How was the party last night?" asked Jessie, coming up the stairs and plonking herself down beside Charley.

"All right," she replied. "Where were you? I didn't see you there."

"Oh, I had to update the website. Lots of photos to add and a blog to write about the opening shows," she explained. Then, leaning closer, she lowered her voice in a conspiratorial tone. "Don't worry, though. I didn't reveal it was *you* who ran onto the stage the first night!"

Charley cringed with embarrassment. Despite her instincts

having been right about the potential threat, she was still regarded as the "guest" who'd freaked out over Ash's performance and stopped the concert.

"I don't blame you for doing it," whispered Jessie. "I know how hard it is. Any time I see Ash, I just want to grab hold of him and never let go." Her eyes took on a faraway glaze. "Still can't believe I'm on his tour bus. It's like a dream come true! So, how did you get invited?"

"My legal guardian knows Ash's manager," Charley replied, hoping the half-truth would be convincing enough. "Which reminds me, I totally forgot to call him back. Will you excuse me?"

"Sure," said Jessie. "I should really call my mom before she thinks Ash has abducted me!" She giggled at the idea. "It took a lot to persuade her to let me come on this tour. I had to promise that I wouldn't do anything stupid."

"Yeah, my guardian warned me to be careful too," said Charley with a rueful smile.

She rose from her seat and headed down the stairs. Seeking some privacy, she found the bathroom cubicle and locked the door. She dialed Blake's number rather than Guardian HQ. It rang for several moments before being picked up.

"Hey!" she said brightly.

There was a slight pause, then a "Hey yourself," followed by silence.

At first Charley thought it was a delay on the line, but the silence became more drawn out. "Are you okay?" she asked.

"You didn't call me back," said Blake.

"Yeah, sorry about that. There was an emergency."

"I guessed as much. That's why I've been worrying all this time."

"Nothing to worry about," said Charley. "Ash had pretended to pass out and tricked me into doing CPR. Turned out to be a tour prank."

Blake snorted. "Sounds like a dumb joke to me. So, how is the almighty Ash? Is he all he's cracked up to be?"

"Truth be told, he's pretty amazing. Having seen him live, I can understand why his fans are so crazy about him."

"Can you now?"

"Don't get jealous!" she cautioned with a laugh. "Ash is way too arrogant for my liking. Besides, he isn't half as cute as you."

"That's good to hear," said Blake, his voice still flat. "I was beginning to think the radio silence meant you'd forgotten me."

"Of course not," she insisted. "Listen, my hunch was right about the laser. There *was* an intruder in the b—"

A knock at the door interrupted her.

"Charley?" called Big T's voice. "We'll soon be arriving in Pittsburgh."

"Okay," she replied. Then in a quieter voice: "Listen, Blake, I've got to go. Missing you."

"Yeah, you too," he said, and cut the call.

Charley stared at her phone, half wishing she hadn't called him. Blake was clearly annoyed she hadn't called back the other day. But what could she do? She was on an assignment. Aside from the routine report-ins, she rarely had time to make social calls. He of all people should understand that. With a sigh, she pocketed her phone. *Long-distance relationships are a nightmare*, she thought.

Charley made her way down the corridor and joined Big T at the front of the bus.

"I hope you're well rested," he said to her. "It's about to get crazy again. I've heard from the security advance party that Ash's hotel is mobbed with fans."

"I'm getting used to that now," replied Charley, gazing through the windshield at the city skyline ahead.

The bus mounted a ramp and approached a monumental golden bridge. Spanning the breadth of the Monongahela River, the bowstring arch structure was an impressive gateway to their next stop on the tour.

"Welcome to Pittsburgh, the City of Bridges!" announced their driver, a grizzled man with a belly the size of a medicine ball.

As they crossed the bridge, following the signs toward

the Pittsburgh arena, Charley glanced up at the lattice of golden steel girders whizzing over their heads.

"Fort Pitt Bridge," said the driver, noting her interest. "Just one of four hundred and forty-six bridges in the city. I bet you're wondering why it's painted gold." He didn't wait for her to answer. "It's to match the city's official colors—black and gold."

Charley nodded and smiled at the talkative driver.

"A very iconic bridge, this one," he said, continuing with his monologue. "Been featured in many films. *Striking Distance, Abduction, The Perks of Being a Wallflower* and even in a video game! This bridge is constructed from over eight thousand tons of steel and—"

A muffled bang rocked the tour bus.

Charley grabbed hold of a handrail as the tour bus suddenly veered across the road. The driver fought to control the wheel. There was another bang and the whole bus shuddered.

Cars honked and swerved at the last second to avoid a collision. Charley clung on for dear life as the bus headed straight for the barrier and the dizzying drop into the river below.

39

Bracing herself for the impact, Charley wished she'd been strapped in by a seat belt. Her only thought was how ironic it would be if, after all the danger she'd faced on assignments, she died in something as mundane as a bus crash.

The barrier came rushing toward them. At the last second, the driver wrenched the wheel hard and steered the bus away from its fatal course. Glancing off the barrier with a screech of metal on metal, the bus swung the other way and careered across four lanes of traffic toward the opposite barrier.

Wrestling with the wheel and working the accelerator and brake, the driver fought to regain control. Despite his efforts, the edge drew ever nearer.

Behind her, Charley heard the other tour members screaming. A passing car was knocked spinning across the lanes. The jolt of the impact was felt through the entire bus, sending people to the floor like bowling pins. Yet still the bus headed toward the drop.

No longer was the Fort Pitt Bridge a welcoming sight. With a crunching of gears, a squeal of brakes and a grating of metal, the bus rocked to an unsteady halt, teetering next to the edge. Below, Charley could see the cold gray waters that would have been their grave.

By some miracle, the driver had managed to stop the bus just in time. Sweat patches staining his white shirt, he let out a shuddering breath and switched off the engine.

"Everyone okay?" asked Big T, hauling himself to his feet.

Charley nodded. She was shaken up but otherwise unhurt. The bassist came staggering down the stairs with Jessie and the drummer, while the others picked themselves up from the floor.

Ash emerged bleary-eyed from his bunk and yawned. "Are we here already?"

Oblivious to their almost-fatal accident, his question prompted a burst of nervous laughter from everyone on board. "Not quite," replied his drummer. "Looks like we might have a bit of a walk ahead."

"Walk?" said Ash. Then he noticed the slight tilt to the tour bus and saw the waters of the Monongahela River outside the window. "Hey, did we crash?"

"No, of course not," said the bassist, his tone sarcastic.

"The driver just thought he'd do an emergency stop on the edge of a bridge!"

Clambering off the bus, Charley joined Big T and the driver to inspect the damage. Her legs were a little shaky. She couldn't believe they'd all escaped the crash with their lives. A few more feet and they would have plunged over the side. The tour bus's front grille was heavily dented from the collision with the car, and the right-hand side was scraped down to the metal.

"Looks like we had a blowout," said the driver, pointing to the nearside front tire. All that was left was a shredded mess of rubber.

"One of your rear tires blew as well," noted Big T. "Surely that's not normal."

"Can happen. Once one tire goes, the others have to bear the load," the driver replied, hunkering down to examine the wheel rims. "We'll have to call a tow truck. This bus ain't going nowhere."

The flash of a camera caught Charley's attention. Gonzo was at the roadside, capturing the accident scene as Ash stepped off the wrecked bus. His lens then focused on the damaged car as the dazed passengers climbed out.

"Hope you've got insurance, Ash!" called Gonzo, snapping away. "Think you might have a personal injury lawsuit on your hands."

"How the hell did Gonzo get here so fast?" exclaimed Charley.

Big T narrowed his eyes at the pap. "Must've been following us."

In the distance the sound of police sirens could be heard.

"Let's get Ash out of here," said Big T, "before this accident scene turns into a publicity nightmare."

40

Expecting a large tour bus, the horde of Ash Wild fans barely gave the yellow taxi a second glance as it pulled up outside the Pittsburgh Hilton Hotel. Then their idol stepped from the vehicle and mayhem ensued. Fans swooped on him with deafening and delighted screams. Instantly he was surrounded and being barraged with requests for photos and autographs.

Ash dutifully signed and posed as Big T tried to keep the crowd at bay and steer him toward the hotel's reception. Charley remained close to Ash, blending in as one of the fans. She was still tense from the bus crash, but this served to heighten her senses, helping her to stay sharp for danger.

She scanned the faces surrounding them, looking for any person who appeared unusually nervous, shifty or out of place. But the fans were so hysterical that it was impossible to tell if anyone posed an actual threat—they *all* looked dangerous.

One girl had her hand deep inside a bag, her eyes glued to Ash. Since most of the crowd were reaching out to the rock star, this girl's behavior seemed odd to Charley. Wondering what she was concealing, Charley positioned herself beside the blond-haired girl. She couldn't see into the bag and tensed in readiness to react at the slightest threat.

As Ash approached, the suspect pulled out . . . a stuffed teddy bear, with a red heart clasped between its paws.

"Ash! This is for you!" she cried, thrusting the toy at her idol.

Accustomed to being showered with gifts by his fans, Ash accepted the bear with good grace and thanked the girl. Charley resumed her surveillance of the crowd. With the teddy bear tucked under his arm, Ash moved on to the next fan. Taking a souvenir concert program from a brown-haired boy, he scribbled his signature across the front.

"What's your name?" Ash asked, to personalize the cover.

"Don't you remember me?" said the fan with a mild look of disappointment.

Ash glanced up and did a double take. So did Charley. There was a distinct familiarity *and* similarity. Charley's alert level shot up.

"It's me, Pete!" said the boy, smiling. "Your 'twin'?"

"You look different . . . or should I say the *same*," remarked Ash.

"Yeah! After what you said, I dyed my hair the same color

as yours," he explained, running a hand through his matching hairstyle. "I also got my ear pierced and contact lenses to match your eyes."

He stared unblinking at Ash so he could show off his dark hazel lenses. The effect was disturbing—like a reflection in a mirror taking on a life of its own. The two boys were practically identical.

Charley instinctively moved in to shield Ash from his self-styled doppelgänger. Other fans noticed the similarity too and began taking photos.

"I'm flattered," said Ash as he handed back the signed program. Then he indicated his left forearm. "You only need my phoenix tattoo now to complete the look."

Big T moved Ash on and through the revolving doors into the hotel.

"Didn't you find that boy a bit creepy?" Charley asked Ash as they entered the relative calm of the hotel's lobby.

Ash shrugged. "That's fan devotion for you."

"But he followed you from New York. Surely that's odd?"

"Not really," he replied. "On any tour I see loads of the same faces."

"But your *own*?" questioned Charley.

"Ash, darling! Are you okay?" cried Zoe, rushing across the lobby toward them. "I heard about the crash. Sounds awful."

"To be honest, I slept through it," he replied.

"Well, let me take that for you." She indicated the teddy bear under his arm. "I'll put it with the rest of the gifts in your room. I have a full schedule of interviews lined up. They'll probably ask about the crash, so I'd better brief you . . ."

As Zoe led Ash away, Charley went to follow, but Big T called her back, indicating for Rick and Vince, two other members of his security team, to keep guard.

"My orders are to stick with Ash," objected Charley.

"He'll be fine for the moment. First, we need to security-check his room."

Crossing the hotel lobby, they entered the elevator and the old bodyguard thumbed the button for the fourth floor. As the elevator slowly ascended, Big T explained, "Hotels throw up a whole host of security issues. First and foremost, we don't have exclusive use. Which means anyone can enter. The hotel doormen will keep the majority of fans out. But with so many entrances and exits, any determined individual can find their way in. And some fans will even get their parents to book them into the same hotel. So stay alert for possible intruders."

"Like that copycat fan?" said Charley. "Should we be worried about him?"

Big T raised an eyebrow. "Granted he's a bit weird, but I wouldn't lose sleep over it. I've witnessed far more obsessive fan behavior in my time. Once a girl turned up to a concert in a wedding dress, hoping Ash would marry her!" He shook his head in wonder. "However, I agree we should keep an eye on the boy. There's a fine line between devotion and stalking."

The doors to the lift pinged open and they stepped out.

Big T checked the floor plan on the wall. "Good. Ash's room is at the end of the corridor."

"Why's that good?" asked Charley.

"Because anyone approaching his suite needs to have a reason to do so," he explained. "If there are rooms beyond, then guests can walk past and this undermines our security."

As they made their way along the corridor, Big T pointed out a red fire-exit sign. "In every hotel we stay in, always locate the two nearest fire exits," he instructed. "Count the doorways, note corridors and any furniture in between, and commit the route to memory. If there's a fire and the corridor's choked with smoke, you'll thank me for it."

Inserting a key card, Big T opened the door to Ash's suite. A luxurious cream-carpeted room spread out before them. There was a walnut desk, coffee table and L-shaped sofa. Through a second doorway lay a king-size bed, wide-screen TV and bathroom with a Jacuzzi. Big T went into the bathroom, checked the shower cubicle, then opened all the closets.

"What are you looking for?" asked Charley.

"Groupies," he said, getting on his knees and peering under the bed.

"Seriously?" asked Charley.

"Along with hidden bugs, cameras and any other sort of surveillance device." Big T took out a small black box from his jacket pocket. The palm-sized unit had two antennae and an LED indicator. Switching it on, he held the device over the telephone on the bedside table.

"Bug detector," he explained. "Know how to use one?"

Charley nodded. "My surveillance tutor showed us a whole bunch of them."

"Good." He tossed her the unit. "Scan the rest of the room while I finish off the physical search."

"Is this necessary every time?" she asked as she slowly swept the device over the pictures, the plug sockets, the lights and every other fixture and fitting in the room.

Big T nodded. "Remember, we're not only protecting Ash's physical safety—we're protecting his privacy too. In my time as a bodyguard, I've come across bugged pens, phone chargers, you name it. I've found fans hiding in closets, paparazzi impersonating cleaning staff, pranksters doing dares. Believe me, I've seen it all!"

41

"Please tell me that was my last interview," said Ash, slumping back in his chair as Big T closed the door on the departing reporter.

Zoe smiled. "Yes, that was your last interview . . . for today at least."

"Thank goodness." Ash rubbed his eyes with the palms of his hands. "My brain's fried."

Charley wasn't surprised. Ash had slogged through ten interviews back-to-back, each reporter asking a variation of the same questions and Ash having to respond to each as if for the first time. A few brought up the "Only Raining" court case with the songwriter Brandon Mills, but most grilled him about the bus crash earlier that morning. Ash's responses were carefully prepared and guided by Zoe to avoid any statements that could be misinterpreted or taken out of context. Charley was now seeing the reality of a superstar's life. There was a lot of hard work behind the success and a lot of media traps to avoid.

Getting up from his chair, Ash went over to the window. "I need to get out. Go for a run or something."

"The hotel has excellent gym facilities," said Zoe helpfully.

"No, I need fresh air. I've been cooped up far too long."

Big T coughed. "Ash, have you seen the crowd outside?"

Ash slid the balcony door open and stepped out. Instantly, an ear-blasting chorus of screams erupted from the street below. Ash gave a quick wave to his fans, causing another torrent of delighted shrieks, before coming back inside.

"Yep," he said with a smirk. "Looks like we'll have to sneak out the back."

Big T regretfully shook his head. "There are fans camped there too. Why not use the gym as Zoe suggested?"

"But I *have* to get out of here!" cried Ash in a surprisingly childish tantrum. He strode through to his bedroom, opened his suitcase and rummaged around for his sneakers and athletic clothes.

"I'm not employed to tell you what you can and can't do," said Big T calmly. "But I'd advise against it."

Ash kicked off his shoes. "I can't be a prisoner of my own fans."

Big T let out a heavy sigh like a steam train coming to a stop. "If you must go for a run, keep a low profile. Otherwise your jog will end up looking like the London marathon!"

"We could leave through the loading bay," suggested Charley, recalling the hotel's layout from the operation folder that José and David had compiled. "It leads to a side street—unlikely any fans would be there."

"And I'll wear my hoodie and sunglasses," said Ash, heading into the bathroom to change.

"Fine," relented Big T. "But Rick and Vince will accompany you." He radioed for the two security guards.

"Aren't you coming?" asked Ash in a teasing tone.

"I'm a tank, not a sports car," Big T replied with good humor. "I'll leave the jogging to the younger pups."

"I'll go too," volunteered Charley.

"As long as you can keep up," called Ash.

Charley held her tongue, reminding herself that actions would speak louder than words. She hurried to her room, almost as eager as Ash to escape the confines of the hotel. Touring wasn't exactly a healthy lifestyle, and she missed her daily runs in the Welsh mountains. She quickly slipped into her running gear and was already waiting outside Ash's door when he emerged.

"Right, let's go," said Ash as Rick and Vince joined them in the corridor.

To avoid detection, the four of them headed down the stairwell to ground level, then worked their way through the kitchens to the loading bay. They got a few stares from the hotel staff but were otherwise unopposed.

"You were right!" said Ash as they walked down the ramp and onto the side street. "No fans at all."

But no sooner had he said this than a figure leaped out from behind a Dumpster. He was armed with a rapid-fire SLR camera and began to reel off shot after shot.

"Trying to sneak out unseen, are we?" said Gonzo, his ratty face triumphant at another exclusive photo. "Running from an accident? That's a criminal act."

Ash kept his hoodie up and his head down. Rick stepped between the camera lens and Ash. "Give it a rest, Gonzo."

"We've all got to make a living," snapped Gonzo. Scuttling ahead to secure a clear shot, he noticed Charley. "So, are you two lovebirds eloping or what?"

"Beat it, Gonzo," said Vince, breaking into a jog with Ash up the street.

"Hey, my name's Gomez!" he spat irritably.

Vince waved him off. "Whatever, Gonzo."

Gonzo now targeted his camera on Charley. "What's your name, *chica*?"

Charley kept a fixed smile on her face and didn't reply, at the same time wondering, *How on earth did he know when and where we'd be coming out?* It was like he had a homing beacon on Ash.

"Not letting your new boyfriend out of your sight, eh?" he continued. "I wouldn't trust him either. Not after how he treated Hanna."

Charley knew the pap guy was trying to bait her, but she had to quash any rumors before they got out of hand and drew too much attention to her. "For the record, I'm *not* his girlfriend."

"Then . . . what are you?" panted Gonzo, struggling to keep up with the group.

"PR," replied Charley, and she raced on.

"And I'm Santa Claus!" he called after her.

Leaving the creep behind, the four runners reached the main road and headed away from the hotel. Charley looked back over her shoulder and saw the horde of fans gathered outside the entrance, still believing their idol was inside. Gonzo emerged from the side street a moment later, puffing and panting. He took a few last photos as they jogged on. Then, leaning against a wall, he lit a cigarette.

"So, where are we going?" Vince asked, running a little ahead of Ash.

"Wherever," he replied. "Just as long as I get some headspace."

Charley glanced at the map on her smartphone, strapped to her upper arm. "Schenley Park is four blocks up, if you like trail running."

"Sounds good." Ash flicked back his hoodie and picked up the pace.

They pounded along the sidewalk, four anonymous runners. But to the trained eye there was a definite formation—Vince a little ahead on Ash's left, Charley on his right and Rick a few paces behind to his left. The subtle positioning provided all-round protection while still remaining low profile.

Ash jogged steadily, only slowing at intersections. No one took much notice of them and they were almost at the park entrance when Vince glanced back to check on Ash, then went down suddenly, hitting the ground hard.

42

Charley saw Vince drop and instinctively shoved Ash sideways into a nearby bus shelter. Believing the bodyguard to have been shot, she kept Ash pinned behind the cover of an advertising sign while her eyes darted around for the shooter.

"Are you all right?" asked Rick, running up to Vince and offering his hand.

"Yes," Vince groaned. "Twisted my ankle, that's all."

"Chill out, Charley!" said Ash, shrugging her off.

Charley relaxed her grip on him. "Sorry," she replied, annoyed at her overreaction.

Ash grinned at her. "Can't keep your hands off me, can you?"

Charley responded with a tight smile. "Remind me to wash them later!"

Rick helped Vince over to the bus shelter's bench. "You

carry on into the park," said Vince, examining his grazed leg and swollen ankle. "I'll wait here until you're done."

"Are you sure?" asked Rick.

"Yeah, just make sure you don't run into any trouble."

Entering through a main gate, the three of them passed an information board. A quick glance at the large map told Charley that the park was a sprawling woodland of hills, valleys and open grass areas. There was a lake to the west, and running trails crisscrossed the park like the roots of a tree. Ash followed the top path that looped across the park's north end, then dropped downslope into a wooded area. Almost immediately the noise of the city was muffled by trees and it felt as if they were deep in the countryside.

"So, you like keeping fit?" asked Ash.

"Sure," replied Charley.

In response Ash increased his pace. Charley sped up to stay by his side. Rick maintained his position several steps behind. The path wound through the woods, across a grassy knoll and past a pond into another woodland. Taking a trail that cut left, they crossed a bridge over a stream and followed a gully through the middle of the park. The pace was fast but easily within Charley's capabilities. They ran steadily, covering three miles in little under half an hour. The fresh air and exercise did wonders for Charley, reinvigorating her and clearing her mind. In hindsight, she didn't regret overreacting to Vince's fall. After all, only the paranoid survive! The question was, why hadn't Rick responded? Was he simply more experienced? Or was he less on the ball?

Passing a sign indicating one mile to the lake, Ash glanced at Charley. "Race you to the lake?"

Charley nodded, up for the challenge. As Ash pulled away, Charley got the sense he wanted to prove something. But she was used to this macho behavior from her bodyguard-training buddies. She lengthened her stride and drew level with him as they followed a trail upslope. The pace was now seriously challenging, and Rick showed signs of flagging, with rapid breathing, a sweat-soaked T-shirt and heavy footfalls.

"Hey!" he panted. "Hold up, you two!"

But Ash and Charley were in the zone and left Rick behind. After a few twists and turns of the path, they completely lost him in the woods. As Ash ran faster, Charley pulled out all the stops to keep up. She was impressed by his fitness, but she shouldn't have been surprised, considering the energy he expended onstage each night—he must run at least half a marathon every performance! As they sprinted along the path, her heart thrummed in her chest, her pulse raced and her breathing quickened. They emerged from the woods with the lake only a few hundred feet ahead. Ash went flat out. Charley pushed herself to her limit, matching Ash stride for stride, as the finish line drew nearer and nearer. Ash was unable to shake her off. They hit the lakeside path together, a result too close to call.

"Well . . . you're certainly fit . . . I'll give you that," Ash panted, bent over double to regain his breath.

"Want to . . . keep going?" asked Charley, hoping he didn't, but aiming to make her point.

Ash glanced up at her, then laughed. "No . . . I need to save *some* energy for tonight." He nodded at a sign pointing to the park cafe. "Besides, I could really go for a drink."

Charley looked behind for Rick. He was nowhere to be seen.

"He'll catch up," said Ash, dismissing the security guard with an exhausted wave of his hand and striding off in the direction of the cafe.

Charley knew Rick would probably be having a fit that he'd lost his Principal. But at least she was still there to guard Ash.

Following the signs to the cafe, they found an empty table outside and sat down. A waitress brought over a menu and they ordered a Coke and a bottle of water.

Ash took a deep draft of his drink, then said, "So, Charley, are you *really* a bodyguard?"

Charley held his gaze. "Are you really a rock star?"

Ash laughed. "Okay, why be a bodyguard then? Seems an odd decision, especially at our age."

"Being a world-famous rock star seems equally odd to me," replied Charley, sipping her water.

Ash nodded. "Fair point. I must admit, it's been a crazy couple of years. Who'd have believed posting a video online would have led to all this? While I wanted to be a musician, I didn't decide to be famous. That just happened. But at some point *you* had to decide to become a bodyguard. Why?"

Charley stared out across the lake. "It's complicated. I'm not sure I even had a decision to make. Certain events in my life took me to this point . . ." She thought back to that fateful day in the coffee shop. *"We cannot change the cards we are dealt, just how we play the hand."*

"What did you say?"

Charley looked at him. "We cannot change the cards we are dealt, just how we play the hand."

"That's a great lyric!" said Ash, grabbing a napkin and trying to get the waitress's attention for a pen. "So, what do your parents think of you being a bodyguard?"

Charley's face clouded. "They're dead . . . but I hope they'd be proud."

"Oh, I'm sorry," said Ash, instantly forgetting his need for a pen. A similar dark cloud settled over Ash's expression. "I understand how you must feel. I'm sure you know, it was in all the papers, but my mum died last year from cancer. And I don't speak to my father. He left me and my mum when I was a baby—so he's pretty much dead to me. Of course, now that I'm rich and famous, he wants to know me! It's Aunt Kay who's been my rock in this whirlwind of fame. She looks out for me now."

"Well, she certainly has your safety as her top priority. Otherwise she wouldn't have contacted Guardian."

Ash nodded, then a frown creased his brow. "Charley, is my aunt telling me *everything*? It's just that after finding out about the pig's blood letter, I question if I'm being told the whole truth. I mean, have I received more death threats that I don't know about? When Vince tripped up on the street, you literally leaped on me like my life depended on it."

"Only the paranoid survive," replied Charley.

"That's Big T's tattoo!" laughed Ash, but his laughter quickly died away and his expression grew dark once more. "He mentioned there might have been an intruder that first night. Am I really in danger on this tour?"

For the first time, Charley saw the scared boy behind the facade of a self-assured, ever-smiling rock star. She thought carefully before answering. "You've got Big T, me and the rest of the security team watching out for you. And, as far as I'm aware, no further threats have been made. But that doesn't mean the threat has gone away. That's why I react the way I do. There are no half measures in this—"

"Excuse me . . . are you Ash Wild?"

Ash looked up into the bright, eager face of a young girl and her friend. He smiled.

"You are, aren't you?" she squealed. "Can I have your autograph?" She held out a paper napkin.

"Sure," said Ash. "Do you have a pen?"

The girl shook her head and there was a moment of panicked dismay. Charley wished she'd brought the pen Amir had supplied, but it wasn't exactly running gear. The girl's friend darted off and grabbed the waitress, who helpfully provided hers, then requested an autograph for herself. As word spread and the excitement grew among the cafe's customers, the two young fans took selfies with Ash on their smartphones. Then they skipped off, thrilled at the chance meeting and instantly sharing their experience online.

"You like the attention, don't you?" said Charley.

"Who wouldn't?" replied Ash, finishing off his drink. "Besides, my fans make me who I am. If I don't give them the time, why should they give me theirs?"

Charley spotted a group of excited girls hurrying along the path toward them. "Well, by the looks of it, a lot more are about to give you their time."

43

"We need to go, Ash," said Charley as more and more fans descended on the cafe.

Wildlings seemed to be materializing from the woods by the dozen. As word spread, girls of all ages swarmed into the park. That was the power of social media: instant communication, instant crowds.

Ash seemed oblivious to the growing numbers. He finished signing a girl's T-shirt, then posed for a photo. Before Charley could pull him away, another girl leaped beside him with a camera and he dutifully smiled.

"Come on!" insisted Charley, taking hold of his arm.

"Hey, I'm next," said a disgruntled fan, shoving Charley aside with an elbow to the ribs.

Briefly, Charley considered dropping the girl with a ridge-hand strike to her neck. But she remembered her unarmed combat instructor's advice: *Any self-defense must be* necessary, reasonable *and* proportional *to the attack*. So Charley waited for the fan to have her photo with Ash before stepping sharply on the girl's toes. A little twist of the heel ensured maximum impact.

"Sorry," said Charley with an apologetic smile as the girl's eyes widened and she gasped in pain.

"Is she all right?" asked a concerned Ash.

"Yes," Charley replied breezily. "Just a little overcome at meeting you."

Leaving the injured fan to limp over to the nearest chair, Charley escorted Ash away from the cafe.

"Gotta go!" called Ash, waving good-bye to his fans.

But that didn't stop them from following him. Like the Pied Piper, Ash led his ever-expanding flock through the park. All the time people snapped away with their cameras, filmed with their phones and demanded autographs. Even as he walked, Ash kept his trademark smile and turned his head toward each and every lens he could: the consummate professional.

"Excuse me! Make way," Charley requested as several fans stood directly in his path.

"Who do you think you are?" challenged one of the girls, squaring up to her.

"Let him through!" ordered Charley, her gaze taking on a steely quality that convinced the girl to step aside.

With ever more fans demanding his attention, Charley had to be Ash's eyes and ears as she shepherded him in the direction of the main gate. But it soon became apparent they'd never reach it. As the woods opened to a grassy area, she spied a mass of people heading their way. The fans waiting at his hotel must have gotten word and rushed the four blocks down to find him. *Where the heck was Rick?* Without him or Vince to back her up, Charley was way out of her depth. She simply didn't have the physical presence or authority to protect Ash among so many people. To those surrounding the rock star she was just another fan.

Charley reassessed their options. If she could get him to the main road, then perhaps they could dive into a taxi and get back to the hotel. "I hope you've got the energy for a final sprint," she whispered to Ash, pointing to a nearby side gate.

She rushed Ash toward the exit. But this only excited the fans more. Like a herd of wildebeest they stampeded across the park, chasing their idol down. Reaching the gate only a few paces ahead of everyone else, Charley burst onto the street with Ash and looked up and down for a taxi . . . but there were none in sight.

As countless fans spilled out of the park and clogged the road, the traffic came to a standstill.

"We love you, Ash!" cried a group of ecstatic girls wearing Wildling Tour T-shirts.

A teenager, waving a banner pronouncing **KIM & ASH 4EVER**, screamed "Marry me!"

"Sign this for my daughter," panted a red-faced middle-aged man, thrusting a notebook into Ash's face.

The barrage of requests and declarations of love were overwhelming and the crush of the crowd quickly turned frightening. Although Ash was used to his fans' hysterical response, without the rock of Big T, he was being tugged and torn like a kite in a storm.

Charley tried to keep hold of him, but she was equally drowning in the sea of people. Her phone vibrated on her arm. A few moments later it rang again, but there was no way she could answer it in the mayhem of the heaving crowd. Paparazzi now jostled shoulder-to-shoulder with the fans, cameras flashing like strobe lights.

"Hey, Ash! Have a good run?" called out Gonzo, his rat face grinning from among the pack.

Suddenly the crowd lurched sideways. Ash stumbled and fell to the pavement. Charley fought to pull him to his feet. His fans, she realized, could be the death of him—trampled and crushed by love.

"Back away!" Charley shouted, dragging Ash to standing and forcing a path through the horde. But mob mentality had taken over. People pushed, shoved, kicked and elbowed to get a glimpse of their idol. No one took any notice of Charley's requests. She now understood why celebrity bodyguards had to be so huge and intimidating. In a crowd like this, nothing but a battering ram would get them through.

"Where's Big T?" cried Ash over the hysterical screaming. His voice was taut with panic as countless hands reached out and pulled at his clothes and hair, everyone trying to get a piece of him.

Charley felt herself losing him to the crowd. She had to find a safe haven. Fast. She spied a bank on the other side of the road and grabbed Ash's hand, hauling him across the street with her. Every step was a battle, like fighting the current of a massive flood. She could feel Ash's hand slipping from her grip.

Then somehow she reached the bank. In a last-ditch effort she shoved Ash through the door, following him. A perplexed security guard rushed up to them.

"Lock the doors!" shouted Charley.

Confronted by a mass of screaming hysterical girls, the guard slammed the doors shut and barricaded them in. The fans clamored at the windows, hundreds of faces pressed up against the glass, peering in at their idol.

Ash collapsed into a chair. "That was beyond crazy!"

"You can say that again," gasped Charley, amazed they'd escaped in one piece. Glancing up at the fan-plastered windows, she was glad the glass was reinforced. Then amid the mayhem she spotted a familiar face. Staring at Ash, his gaze unwavering, Pete raised a bandaged arm and smiled. The smile sent a small shiver through Charley—it was like a ghost copy of Ash's trademark grin.

"So, where do we go from here?" asked Ash, oblivious to his stalker clone.

"Well, there's always the vault!" Charley half joked as she took out her cell phone and saw she had multiple missed calls from Big T. Guessing he was worried about Ash's whereabouts, she immediately called him back for an emergency pickup.

44

"You two clowns are about as useful as an inflatable dart-board!" bellowed Big T, the tendons in his thick neck bulging so much that he looked like he might burst a blood vessel.

Charley stood motionless as the veteran bodyguard vented his fury.

"I put you in charge of the *single most important person* on this tour and you blew it!" he barked, wagging a gnarled finger at Vince and Rick. "One of you princesses sprains an ankle, while the other can't run a mile without having a heart attack! The very least I expect from my security team is that they be fit, effective and competent. Qualities neither of you seem to possess."

The two security guards stared shamefaced at the carpet as their boss laid into them.

Big T pointed his finger at Charley. "If it wasn't for this young lady here, Ash would likely be in the hospital now or worse. You two excuses for bodyguards are on night shift for the next week! Now get out of my sight!"

Vince and Rick scurried out of Big T's hotel room, their tails between their legs, simply grateful not to have been fired on the spot.

"And what are you looking so smug about?" snapped Big T, turning on Charley.

She stiffened and swallowed nervously.

"I called you *five* times! Why in the world didn't you answer?"

"I—I was busy protecting Ash," she explained, stumbling over her words. "I didn't see the missed calls . . . until I got to the bank."

"You stopped at a bloody cafe for a drink! You had more than enough opportunity to report in before the situation got out of hand. Next time you're solo, call in *immediately*. You're not some Katniss Everdeen. You may be trained as a bodyguard, but you're still just one girl! And an inexperienced one at that."

Chastened by his stern words, Charley bowed her head and fell silent. She had hoped for some praise for her actions, but deep down she knew that Big T was right. She'd ignored one of the basic principles of close protection: constant communication. She should have reported their location and status.

Big T continued to glare at her, the vein above his left

temple throbbing. Then his fierce expression eased a little and he let out a heavy sigh. "That said, you made the best of a bad situation. Holing up in a bank was smart thinking. And at the end of it all, Ash is unharmed, if a little shaken."

Charley allowed herself to breathe again.

"The press, though, is going to have a field day that Ash was in public without apparent security." Big T ran a hand over his wrinkled dome. "And Ms. Gibson will have my guts for garters over it!"

"I'm sorry, Big T. I just didn't expect so many fans to turn up so quickly."

"Always expect the unexpected," stated Big T, echoing Colonel Black's own words of advice during her training. "In the future, heed the patron saint of bodyguards: Murphy's Law."

Charley frowned. She noticed the same words tattooed on his neck. "Murphy's Law?"

"Anything that can go wrong, will go wrong," Big T explained. "Now get some rest before tonight's concert. I have a nasty feeling that Murphy might make another appearance."

Charley headed to her room, then stopped at the door. "Speaking of Murphy's Law, there's one thing still bothering me."

"What's that?" asked Big T.

"How did Gonzo know Ash would exit through the loading bay?"

Big T shrugged. "Luck, probably. He hangs out in all the sewers."

Charley shook her head. "No. He was lying in wait. He knew."

Big T furrowed his brow. "How, Sherlock? We swept Ash's room, remember, and it was all clear."

Charley thought for a moment. "Either someone told him or . . . I missed a bug during the surveillance sweep."

Going over to the large desk in his room, Big T picked up the bug detector. "Only one way to find out."

Ash was down in the hotel lobby, chilling with the rest of the band in the VIP lounge, so his suite was empty. Big T let himself in with a spare key card. Charley closed the door behind them and they began a second security sweep of the room.

Big T ran the detector over the TV, phone, plug sockets, pictures, lights and every nook and crevice of the suite. But the LED indicator stayed resolutely green.

He glanced up at the ceiling. "Did you check the smoke detector?"

"No," Charley admitted. "I don't think so."

He held the device up to the white plastic casing. The LED indicator didn't even flicker.

Big T looked at Charley. "Maybe we do have a snitch among the team."

Then Charley's eyes were drawn to the pile of flowers and

gifts on the central table. "These weren't here when we did the security sweep the first time."

Big T handed her the detector. She swept the device over the various bouquets, boxes of chocolates and cuddly toys. As the sensor passed a teddy bear clutching a heart, it buzzed in her hand and the indicator shot into the red. Big T picked up the suspect bear and examined it. He tugged on the black bead of its left eye. The eyeball popped from its socket to expose a camera lens attached to a transmitter. In its ear he discovered the tiny bud of a microphone.

"Very sneaky, Gonzo!" growled Big T, before ripping the bear's ear off.

45

The glass-fronted Pittsburgh arena, usually the host venue for ice-hockey matches and basketball games, had been transformed into a fifteen-thousand-seat concert hall. Ash's unique guitar-shaped stage had been installed the day before and the immense speaker stacks and complex lighting rig rapidly constructed overnight. Fans who'd arrived early were already filtering into the arena and there was a buzz of anticipation in the air.

Charley hung backstage. Ash was secure in his dressing room, preparing himself for the gig. Big T had instructed Charley not to tell him about the teddy-bear spy cam they'd found. "It doesn't represent a threat, merely an irritation," he'd explained. After her conversation with Ash at the cafe, though, Charley wondered if it was right to withhold that information from the target himself. She found Big T by the coffee machine in the artists' lounge and questioned this decision.

"There's no point worrying Ash unnecessarily," said Big T, pouring himself a double espresso. "He needs to focus on performing. It's *our* job to worry on his behalf."

"But I've only just started building his trust. I don't want to break it."

Big T took a sip of coffee and grimaced at its bitter taste. "Hey, imagine if the president of the United States was told about every threat to his life. The poor guy would be a gibbering wreck by the end of the week. Ash is on a need-to-know basis. For his own good."

"What if our assumption is wrong?" pressed Charley. "What if the teddy bear wasn't planted by Gonzo?"

"Who else could it be? Motive and circumstance point to Gonzo. Granted, the girl who gave Ash the bear might be an infatuated fan wanting to spy on her idol, but those devices cost a ton. We're not talking pocket money here."

"How about the maniac who's been sending Ash the death threats?" suggested Charley. "He could have bribed, persuaded or even *threatened* the girl to do it."

"You assume the maniac's a guy," said Big T, raising a world-weary eyebrow. "Unless we see that girl again, we won't know one way or the other. Whoever's to blame, our response is the same. We tighten security around Ash. Which reminds me, I need to check in with the venue manager about the corporate boxes. Murphy's Law and all that."

He drained his espresso and headed out of the lounge.

Charley followed Big T into the corridor. One member of the security team was stationed outside Ash's dressing-room door. With her Principal secure, Charley took a walk backstage to familiarize herself with the new venue. She noted the fire exits and quickest routes to each. Passing various road crew and sound technicians, her eyes flicked to their photo passes, checking that everyone had one. As she approached the main stage, Charley's attention was caught by a shadowy figure dropping down from one of the lighting rig's wire-rope ladders next to the backstage curtains. This behavior seemed odd and out of place compared to the rest of the crew, and she immediately went on the alert. Heading over to where the person had disappeared, she pulled back the drape to discover Jessie crouching in the darkness behind the drum riser.

Jessie flinched and looked shocked. "You startled me!" she exclaimed, resting a hand on her heart.

"What are you doing?" asked Charley.

She responded with a guilty smile. "I can't resist peeking out on the stage before a concert. It's fabulous! This is exactly what Ash sees each night." Jessie stepped aside and invited her to climb the ladder. "Go on, take a look yourself."

Clambering up a few rungs, Charley peered over the top of the riser. The stage rolled out before her, its catwalk guitar neck protruding deep into the audience. With the venue lights on, she could see thousands upon thousands of fans gathering in the stalls, their excited chatter echoing around the vast arena. She glanced up at the mega-video screens running preconcert footage, then at the lighting rig high above, where she spied the tiny figure of a spotlight operator moving among the struts.

"Cool, isn't it?" said Jessie.

Charley nodded and dropped back down. "I don't know how Ash has the courage to step out and perform in front of a huge crowd like that."

"It's because he's a god," Jessie replied reverentially. She crept through the curtain. "I'll catch you later. The concert's going to start soon."

"Don't forget your bag," said Charley, noticing a small backpack on the floor, partly hidden by the curtain's black fabric.

"That's not mine. But thanks anyway."

Jessie disappeared around the corner.

Charley bent down to pick it up. Then stopped herself. Something about it made her think twice.

She spotted a guitar technician nearby. "Is this yours?" she asked, pointing to the suspect bag. The long-haired technician shook his head and went back to fine-tuning the row of electric guitars. Charley asked another crew member, but it wasn't his either.

Charley reminded herself of the rule of the Four Cs: *confirm, clear, cordon, control.*

She had to confirm her suspicions first.

A bearded roadie, whom Charley vaguely recognized from rehearsals, came down the ladder. She asked if he knew who the backpack belonged to. He grunted a no and carried on. Charley asked several more people, but no one laid claim.

If you can't find the owner, then the item must be considered a threat, Bugsy had said.

Charley bent down and gave the bag a sniff. There was the faintest aroma of almonds. Charley decided it was time to alert Big T. She was about to call him on her radio when Bugsy's voice sounded in her head again: *Radio waves are often used to trigger remote-control bombs!*

Charley immediately switched off her phone and comms unit, then dashed away to find Big T.

46

"We should clear the area, at the very least," Charley insisted as she stood with Big T and the tour manager at a wary distance from the suspect backpack.

"How can you be certain it's a bomb?" asked Terry, peering at it in the dim light of backstage.

"I can't," replied Charley. "But so far no one's claimed it and I smelled almonds, which could mean plastic explosives."

Terry spoke into his radio. "Attention, all crew. Has anyone lost a backpack?"

Charley instinctively flinched. But the bag didn't explode. *Well, at least that's been cleared up*, she thought. *The bomb isn't triggered by radio waves.*

Big T turned to the tour manager. "Anyone respond?"

Terry shook his head. "What do we do now?"

"As Charley said, clear the area," replied Big T. "Get Ash off the premises."

"But the concert!" Terry exclaimed. "It's due to start any minute now."

"Not with Ash, it isn't," said Big T, directing two security guards to immediately move people out of the vicinity. Shocked at the news of a bomb, the technicians and road crew dropped what they were doing and headed to the exit on the direction of the guards.

"But we can't just cancel the gig over a lost backpack!" Terry argued as Big T sent word to evacuate Ash at once.

"With the death threats made against Ash," argued the bodyguard, "we must assume the worst-case scenario."

"Why can't we just look inside the darn bag?" said Terry, walking over to it.

"NO!" said Charley, grabbing his arm. "It could be booby-trapped."

Terry held up his hands in frustration. "It's just a bag!"

"A bag that *could* be a bomb," said Big T. "We need to call the authorities."

"And how long's that going to take?" Terry shrugged off Charley's hand and marched over to the backpack.

"Don't!" warned Big T, moving rapidly away from the suspected bomb.

Terry bent down to open the bag. Big T pushed Charley behind a transport crate, then dived for cover himself. There was a long, deafening silence.

Then Terry appeared, holding a can of soda, an open pack-age of mixed nuts and a sandwich box in his hand. "Some bomb," he said, glaring at Charley and Big T crouched on the ground. "For heaven's sake, Big T, keep that girl of yours on a leash! She's going to be the death of this tour."

The manager strode off in a fury and started barking or-ders to get the concert back on schedule.

"Sorry," said Charley, feeling like she'd let Big T down again.

"Nothing to be sorry about," he replied, lumbering back to his feet. "You alerted me. I take responsibility thereafter. Besides, it's better to be safe than blown to bits! Even if the bomb does turn out to be a moldy cheese sandwich." He grunted a laugh.

Charley was grateful for Big T's good humor, but she knew she'd screwed up *again*. "You were right to call me in-experienced. On this assignment, I feel like I'm always cry-ing wolf."

"And one day there might be a wolf," said Big T. "As a bodyguard, you have to suspect everything and everyone. *Guilty until proven innocent* is my motto."

"I thought it was *Only the paranoid survive*."

"Depends on which arm I look at," replied Big T, showing her the opposite forearm with a tattoo of a pair of weighted scales and the words *guilty until proven innocent* inscribed beneath it. "Now, don't lose faith in yourself. Ash has a gig to do and you need to be on the ball."

With the emergency over, the crew and technicians hurriedly returned to their duties. Everyone was under pressure to make up for lost time.

"Don't forget," said Big T as he headed to Ash's dressing room. "Murphy's Law applies at all times."

Charley nodded. She was now a full convert to Murphy and his Law. Anything that could go wrong for her on this assignment seemed to be doing exactly that! She took up her position at the side of the stage as instructed by Big T, only too happy to comply since it allowed her to keep a low profile. Her name had to be dirt among the crew after a second false alert.

Jessie ran up to her. "Did you hear there was a suspected bomb threat?" she gasped.

Charley nodded and said nothing.

"I never imagined a tour could be so *dangerous*," remarked Jessie, her tone suggesting excitement rather than fear at the idea.

The house lights suddenly went dark and the video screens began a countdown. Fifteen thousand fans yelled along with it: *"FIVE . . . FOUR . . . THREE . . . TWO . . . ONE!"*

A huge explosion shuddered through the arena . . .

But Charley didn't flinch. She knew this explosion was all part of the show. Fireworks lit up the stage in a waterfall of red and gold sparks, and a pounding heartbeat throbbed from the speakers at a gut-thumping volume. Images of a winged boy flashed across the video screens, his silhouette leaping from frame to frame as a blazing fire took hold and raced after him. The fierce crackle of burning grew louder and louder as the winged boy was surrounded, then consumed by flames.

Out of the heart of the raging fire, a single word pulsed in time to the dying beat of the music.

INDESTRUCTIBLE.

The word shone like a beacon, then morphed into *IMPOSSIBLE?*

Before transforming one final time . . . *I'M POSSIBLE!*

A thunderclap burst from the speakers and Ash shot up from a toaster lift in the floor. He landed on the stage with the grace of an eagle. Behind him on the video screens, a flaming phoenix burned bright.

Ash pumped a fist in the air. "What's up, Pittsburgh!"

The arena erupted with screams and cheers. Picking up his guitar, he struck a chord that started the blistering riff of his first hit, "Easier."

Out of the darkness, a large missile-like object plummeted from above. Charley glimpsed it only at the very last second as it flashed past the central screen. There was no time to react.

The spotlight dropped from the lighting rig like a meteor.

It smashed into the stage right where Ash was standing. Knocked off his feet by the impact, he crumpled to the floor. The audience fell deathly silent as their idol lay motionless among the debris of shattered glass, splintered wood and twisted metal.

47

"Tell me what happened," demanded Kay. Her green eyes blazed with emotion on the computer screen. Despite it being two in the morning in the UK, she still managed to look glamorous on the video chat. Yet the news about Ash had visibly shocked her, and her face was porcelain white.

"It was an accident," explained Terry, seated beside Big T in his hotel room. "The clamp securing the spotlight failed."

"What about the safety cable?" said Kay. "Shouldn't that have stopped the light from falling?"

Terry swallowed uneasily. "For some reason, it wasn't attached."

"*Not attached!*" Kay exclaimed, her familiar tiger spirit returning. "That doesn't sound like an accident to me."

In the context of Ash's death threats, Charley was compelled to agree. But she kept her opinion to herself as she sat quietly with Zoe, the publicity executive, on the edge of the bed.

"There's no evidence that the light was tampered with," replied Big T.

"Then how could it happen?"

Terry wiped a hand over his dry mouth. "We were in a rush to set everything up. The safety cable was likely over-looked."

Even across a divide of four thousand miles, everyone felt the ferocity of Kay's glare.

"As you know, the crew is always under pressure to set up for each gig," Terry hurriedly explained. "But even more so when a false bomb alert delays the already tight schedule."

Kay's smooth brow wrinkled slightly. "What bomb alert?"

Terry directed an accusing stare at Charley. "That's down to your *guest* here."

With openmouthed dismay, Charley realized the tour manager was trying to shift the blame for the incident onto her. "I don't see how that has anything to do with it," she protested.

"It has *everything* to do with it," he insisted.

"Hang on, what about that man I spotted in the lighting rig before the concert? Perhaps he's responsible? Maybe it wasn't an accident at all."

"Enough of your paranoid assertions!" said Terry. "That

could only have been Joel, one of my most reliable roadies. And he'd have been able to complete his checks properly if you hadn't raised the alarm over a lunch box!"

"The backpack *could* have been a bomb," argued Charley.

"But it wasn't, was it?" countered Terry, glowering at her.

Charley knew she was being made a scapegoat for his road crew's mistakes, and this time Big T wasn't stepping to her defense. But she realized he could only put his neck on the line so many times.

Then Big T broke his silence. "Pointing the finger doesn't change what happened. The most important thing at the moment is Ash."

"Quite true," said Kay from the computer screen. "How is he doing?"

Zoe leaned toward the webcam with a reassuring smile. "He's recovering fast. Like the song goes, he's indestructible!"

"Ash got away with only a few cuts and bruises," explained Big T. "If he'd landed onstage from the toaster lift even one step farther back, though, the spotlight would have crushed him."

"That doesn't bear thinking about." Kay sighed. "Where is he now?"

"In his room, sleeping," said Big T.

Terry pinched the bridge of his nose and rubbed his weary eyes. "We had to cancel the concert, of course."

"What about the rest of the tour?" asked Kay. "Is Ash able to continue?"

Terry gave a nod. "The doctor says he's physically fine. So I don't foresee any problem."

"Yes, but the question is, does he *want* to?"

48

The atmosphere on the repaired tour bus the following day was subdued. Ash had holed himself up in the back lounge, making it clear he didn't want to be disturbed. The next stop on the tour was Columbus, Ohio, and as far as everyone knew, the concert was going ahead. But there was deep concern among the band and crew whether Ash was in the right state of mind to perform.

"So, apart from being withdrawn, is he otherwise okay?" José asked Charley during the conference call to Guardian HQ. José was the go-to for any medical issues during Operation Starstruck. Blake and David were also on the line.

"I think so. I haven't had much chance to chat with him," said Charley. She was in the toilet cubicle, as had become her custom to ensure some privacy when reporting in. "As I understand it, Ash is more upset for his fans that the concert was canceled. But he does seem a lot quieter than usual."

"I guess it's pretty traumatic if a ninety-pound spotlight almost crushes you to death!" snorted Jason.

"It was certainly a close call," replied Charley coolly.

"Jody says he's probably in mental shock, like after a car crash," continued José. "Hang on, she just handed me a list of symptoms . . . Okay, it says here that he may swing between bouts of depression, anxiety, anger, despair, hyperactivity and withdrawal. But the symptoms usually resolve themselves in a few days or so."

"Thanks, José, that's good to know. I'll keep an eye out for them."

"You worried about him?" asked Blake. These were the first words he'd spoken since she'd reported in.

"Of course I am," she replied. "That's my job."

"I know," he shot back a little too quickly. "I meant whether you thought he was becoming unstable. I've heard rock stars can be a little unhinged."

No, you didn't, she thought, guessing exactly what he was pushing at. Charley was growing tired of Blake's jealousy and snippy remarks every time she reported in. Either he was short with her, mistrusting or simply in a bad mood. She understood that it was hard on them being apart for so long. And difficult to find the time to resolve any issues. But if he couldn't trust her, then what was the point in them dating?

"So, Charley, have you faced any more crowds single-handedly?" asked David when she went quiet.

"We all saw the news footage of Ash being mobbed by his fans, supposedly without protection," remarked José. "Can't believe you got him out of that situation alive!"

"Me neither—" Through the wall of the toilet cubicle she heard an anguished cry, then a loud bang. "Gotta go!"

Ending the call, Charley rushed out into the corridor. Her first thought was that it was another tire blowout. Then she heard a crash and splintering of wood from the back lounge. She burst through the door to find Ash furiously smashing his acoustic guitar on the floor.

The body cracked. The strings twanged. And the neck snapped.

"Ash! What are you doing?" cried Charley, stunned to see him destroying one of his most prized guitars.

Ash tossed the shattered instrument to the ground, then stamped on the broken remains.

"You useless piece of junk!" he cried as his foot went through the guitar's body. His fit of fury eventually ebbed away and he slumped back into the sofa, sobbing with his head in hands.

Cautiously, Charley approached, sat down next to him and put an arm around his heaving shoulders.

"I—I . . . can't write anymore," he cried, hitching in a ragged breath. "I've . . . lost the songs. I—I can't hear them anymore . . ."

Charley patiently listened to his distress, realizing this

was the mental shock Jody had diagnosed. He trembled uncontrollably and she gently held him in her arms. Jessie popped her head around the door, a concerned look on her face. Charley held up a hand to say all was okay and to give them some space. With a small nod, Jessie quietly retreated from the room.

As Charley waited for Ash's sobs to subside, she spotted his laptop open on the table. A mostly blank page had the beginnings of a song that was stalled on the first line: *You lift me up because . . .*

In an open smaller browser window was a feed from Ash's social media site. A stream of well-wishers were posting messages of support following the previous night's canceled concert. Interspersed between these, like poisonous thorns on a berry bush, were acid comments from haters either joking about the near tragedy or wishing the spotlight *had* hit him. Charley disregarded these.

"Judging by your fans' response, they love your songs and you," she told him. "I'm sure you haven't lost your touch. You're just in shock and a little stressed out at the moment, that's all."

Ash looked up at her with reddened eyes. "B-but writing songs is all I know. It's who I am. It's *why* my fans like me. I'm terrified my muse won't come back."

"Of course it will," Charley assured him. "If you can write a song like 'Only Raining,' you're born with the gift."

This only made Ash sob again.

He eventually regained control of his emotions. "But w-what if it doesn't come back? I've tried everything I know. Nothing seems to break the block. Ever since that letter bomb, I've been struggling. I can't sleep. I have nightmares about it. I just don't understand why anyone would hate me that much. What have I done to them?"

Charley thought about the man who'd snatched Kerry all those years ago. And of the terrorists who'd hijacked the plane her parents had been on. Tears now threatened to come to her eyes. "There are people out there who hurt and hate for no reason but their own. It's not your fault. You've done nothing wrong."

"Then why is someone trying to kill me?"

"Last night was just an accident, like the bus crash," assured Charley. She pointed to his computer screen. "You have to ignore the haters and focus on those who love you. Besides your band, crew, Big T and your aunt, you have a whole legion of fans supporting you. They'll inspire you. You just need to give it time."

Ash nodded. "You're right," he said, wiping his nose with the sleeve of his sweatshirt. "Not much of a rock star, am I? You must think I'm pathetic for crying like a baby."

"I certainly don't! We all have to cry sometimes," replied Charley.

Ash managed a weak smile. "You should be a lyricist."

His laptop pinged as a new message came in. A photo appeared in the browser window of Ash onstage, the blur of a falling spotlight just behind his head.

The caption beneath read:

`Accidents don't just happen.`

The Next Pulse-Pounding Adventure
Is Available in Bookstores Now!

Turn the Page for a Sneak Peek at

Book 8: Traitor

Pete was as jittery as any one of the twenty thousand Wildling fans packed into Columbus's Nationwide Arena. Perhaps even more so because he knew what was coming.

This time he'd managed to get a standing ticket and, after a fair bit of pushing and shoving, was in prime position right beside the neck of the guitar stage. The atmosphere in the arena was highly charged. After the tragic and abrupt end to the Pittsburgh show, Ash's fans were even more desperate to see him. Rumors had been flying that the concert would be canceled at the last minute, and a barely suppressed panic had spread among the audience. Some fans had even resorted to praying in groups for Ash's delivery onto the stage.

Thirty minutes later than scheduled, the house lights dimmed and the countdown began.

The audience screamed in delight. Pete enthusiastically joined in with the countdown, barely able to hear himself above the noise. His gut tightened as the opening explosion rumbled from the speakers, and he had to shield his eyes from the blinding cascade of red and gold sparks. His own heart seemed to beat in unison with the intro's rhythm. Then he felt a rush of exhilaration as the winged silhouette flitted from screen to screen before being consumed by flames.

INDESTRUCTIBLE . . . IMPOSSIBLE? . . . I'M POSSIBLE!

Ash shot up from the toaster lift and landed on the stage. *Not as perfectly as in New York,* thought Pete, *but still an impressive entrance.*

Immediately Ash took two strides forward before thrusting a fist into the air. "What's up, Columbus?"

The audience roared their approval, relieved and overjoyed to see their idol. After a swift, almost unconscious glance upward, Ash struck the opening chord to "Easier," and the band kicked in.

Pete sang along to every word. He watched Ash dance across the stage, his eyes never wavering from his idol. Even after a couple of shows, Pete was beginning to recognize some of his routines. But he could tell Ash wasn't as self-assured as in previous gigs. His performance seemed a little "tight," and every so often, the rock star would look nervously up at the lighting rig. That was to be expected, though, considering Pittsburgh.

Pete's arm started itching. He tried not to scratch the

scabbing skin underneath the bandage. Otherwise he'd damage his new tattoo.

Midway through the gig, a dark-haired girl with freckles stood on his foot. She was thirteen, maybe fourteen, and chewing gum voraciously. She shot him an apologetic smile, then did a double take. The girl opened her mouth and said something. But Pete couldn't hear her over the noise of the band and screaming fans. He leaned closer, and she shouted in his ear, "I said, you look just like Ash. Has anyone told you that before?"

"No," he replied, shaking his head.

"Well, you do!"

Pete grinned. He'd made an extra-special effort to resemble his hero. He'd even managed to find some clothes that matched the ones Ash wore. And it pleased him every time some fan mentioned the similarity.

All through the next set of songs, Pete was aware that the girl kept sneaking peeks at him. She'd "bump" against him, her bare arms touching his. With so many people crowded around, it was impossible not to be in contact with one another, but the girl seemed to be doing it on purpose. He caught her eye and responded with the Ash Wild trademark smile he'd been practicing every night in the mirror. She coyly looked away, but remained close.

As the girl continued to flirt with him, Pete thought to himself that he would *kill* to have Ash's life.

ACKNOWLEDGMENTS

Launching a book series is a team effort and I couldn't have hit the "target" without:

Brian Geffen, my editor at Philomel Books—thank you for all the editorial sharpshooting and endless enthusiasm.

Michael Green, Publisher, for making the Bodyguard series such a priority and ensuring that the books hit the bull's-eye!

Robert Farren, my copy editor, for never hesitating to pull the trigger on any editorial queries.

And most important of all, my readers for cheering the series on and telling the world about it.

Read, enjoy and stay safe!
—Chris

Any fans can keep in touch with me and the progress of the Bodyguard series on my Facebook page, or via the website at www.bodyguard-books.com.